The Proclaimers

A drunken dispute between two young cowboys ends in a violent death. What follows is a vengeful father's spiteful desire for retribution by making a public proclamation that he will pay $10,000 to any person who will give him justice. However, a jury has acquitted the young man who shot his son of any wrongdoing.

The family attorney, who was tasked to raise the proclamation that seeks Biblical justice of an eye for an eye, is so horrified by this vindictive act that he takes it upon himself to save the father from his own despicable behaviour. He enlists the help of Walter Garfield – a man whom some would say is well past his prime. But while Walt may be getting a little old and more than a little cantankerous, he is still a man of the Old West.

As the last days of the nineteenth century come to a close, maybe, just maybe, this old ex-marshal is the only one who can save the young cowboy from those who will kill on sight just to get their hands on the vast reward that is on offer by proclamation. . . .

By the same author

Raking Hell
No Coward

For more information about the author
please visit: www.leeclinton.com

The Proclaimers

Lee Clinton

A Black Horse Western

ROBERT HALE · LONDON

ISBN 978-0-7198-0792-3

Robert Hale Limited
Clerkenwell House
Clerkenwell Green
London EC1R 0HT

www.halebooks.com

Typeset by
Derek Doyle & Associates, Shaw Heath
Printed and bound in Great Britain by
CPI Antony Rowe, Chippenham and Eastbourne

For Max

1

A SQUEEZE OF A TRIGGER

In a thunderclap of sound a shot is fired to explode and propel a small lead bullet, no bigger than the tip of a woman's finger, down a short spiralled barrel towards its target. The projectile is shot from a polished brass case locked within a revolving steel chamber and accelerates to a speed of close to 1,000 feet per second, spinning straight and level. It is a once only flight that will last no more than a second. A journey of physical practicality – no moral conscience here, no hate, no thought of retribution or vengeance. Such emotions belong to the firer, the one who pulls, jerks or deliberately and slowly squeezes the trigger. But now unleashed, that shot cannot be recalled and it will strike whatever lies in its deadly path. If it punches into the smooth rounded bone of the skull to enter into the soft grey centre of the brain, then death will be almost instantaneous. If it strikes a limb it will tear flesh, shatter bone and pulverize muscle. If it thumps into the body, the chest or stomach, it will more than likely rip into a vital organ and cause immediate and immense bleeding. To the victim, the impact of such a wound to the body will feel like the steel punch of an invisible fist.

The first and immediate response to such a body blow is one

of surprise, often accompanied by an expletive. It is a shocked and unbelieving curse, followed by the compulsion to examine the small round dark puncture that hides the mass of ruptured vessels, where pools of dark blood now begin to puddle, then flow from the entry and exit wounds like a leaking tap.

The body reacts with instinct in order to survive, by redirecting blood from other parts to rush to the wound in a futile effort to help. Shock quickly follows as blood drains from the limbs and face, turning the skin to a pallid ashen colour and the lips to a purple hue. A mantle of icy-cold descends over the poor unfortunate as his lips begin to quiver then tremble uncontrollably. The loss of blood makes death inevitable, but there is no immediate haste to that final crossing. The brain, now in a state of severe shock, spins uncontrollably back through a lifetime of memories, to be followed by a calm that is mixed with a terrible feeling of futility and loneliness. The final words spill from the lips of the dying and it is inevitably a call for a mother.

So it was for the young man who lay upon the rough timber floor of the Silver Eagle Saloon, his head close to the spittoon and brass bar rail, surrounded by onlookers who would remember this day; this scene; this moment for a lifetime. Before them lay the consequence and waste of a brief dispute, too much liquor and the deadly exchange of gunfire.

'Get the town doctor,' comes the call from one of the onlookers.

'No need,' is the reply from the old man who is leaning in close to hear the dying man's final words. 'He's gone,' he says. 'Get the undertaker instead.'

2

MODERN TIMES

The sheriff had a splitting headache and the piercing ring of the double brass bell upon the newly installed telephone hadn't helped.

'Do you want me to go?' The deputy knew the sheriff was suffering. He'd seen it before. 'I can look after this one.'

'No. It's a killing. I better see, but I need you to come along and assist. You can then finish up any of the paperwork, because as soon as we are done I'm going to lie down.'

'What do we need?' asked the deputy.

'A clear head,' said the sheriff as he lifted his hat from the peg, 'and a set of shackles. We may need to bring the shooter in if he hasn't done a runner.'

'Rifle?'

'That too.' The sheriff closed his eyes tight and willed his head to overcome the pain he was feeling just behind the eyes. But it didn't work. 'Daylight,' he said as he opened his eyes.

'What?' said the deputy as he pulled the silver-grey handcuffs from the drawer below the rifle cabinet.

'It's still daylight,' repeated the sheriff. 'Haven't had a killing in over two years and that was at night, late. This one was done in daylight.'

'Does it matter?'

'No, not really. But someone has the time and money to drink themselves silly during the day when they should be out working. So what does that mean?'

'Lazy moneyed-up cowboys?'

'You would think so.'

'Sheriff Ireland,' said the undertaker, nodding with deference to acknowledge the arrival of the law.

The sheriff nodded back. 'Clem,' he said, pushing his hat back a little to touch the left temple with two fingers, before looking around the bar at the patrons who stood in sombre silence. 'You'll get yourself a reputation beating the law to the body,' he said softly, before addressing the small crowd. 'Has anyone left? Done a runner?'

'I've got a telephone now,' whispered the undertaker. 'Stan called me. Near rang it off the wall, he was so excited.'

The barman came out from behind the bar and towards the sheriff. 'We're all here, everyone who was in the bar when the shooting occurred. No one has left.'

Some heads in the crowd nodded in agreement.

'Everyone? Including the shooter?'

'Yes, he's over there.' The barman nodded towards a young man standing close to the end of the bar, erect with a glazed look of disbelief on his face.

'The body?'

'Still where it fell. He died real quick. Had just a few brief words. Looks like he was shot in the heart.'

'Let's take a look. After you, Clem. You come too, Stan.'

The undertaker led the way as the sheriff and the barman followed. The crowd parted, clearing a path to the feet of the deceased.

'Name?'

The undertaker responded. 'Tambling, so I've just been told.'

'Age?'

'Twenty-one,' said the bartender, interjecting quickly.

The sheriff raised his eyes just a little. The face was that of a youth not much over eighteen.

'Where is he from?'

There was silence.

'Anyone?' The sheriff made the call over his shoulder to the crowd of onlookers.

'East. Pennsylvania.'

Sheriff Ireland turned to see a cowboy standing in the front row of onlookers, who was pulling a red bandanna from his neck. 'And you?'

The young man now seemed reluctant to speak, hesitating until he finally stammered, 'Jim, James, James Keap.' He licked a dry bottom lip.

'You know this man?' The sheriff glanced down at the body.

'Sort of. I met him last week. We are staying at the same boarding house. The Windsor on Efrin Street.'

'Is Tambling his first or last name?'

'Last. It's Morris. Morris Tambling. Morris Wilfred Tambling.'

'And you were here when it happened?'

'Yes. Yes I was.' The words didn't come with any great conviction or enthusiasm.

'You saw it happen?'

The cowboy nodded.

'As a witness I will need you to make a statement.'

Keap, who was also not much over eighteen, nodded again slowly as he gazed at the body and continued to lick his bottom lip.

'Were you two on your own or travelling with others when you came in here?'

'No, just the two of us. Together. We came in around noon.'

'Anyone else see this happen?' The sheriff called to the small gathering.

Most raised their hands.

'I'm only interested in those who actually saw the shooting first hand.'

Most of the arms lowered.

'I will be taking witness statements and you may be required to testify in a court of law.'

All but two hands dropped quickly.

The sheriff looked at the volunteers. The first he knew, Harry Burrell, and was surprised to see him, as he was sure he was a pledge man. The second he also knew, but only by the nickname of Silver. He was an old miner who hung around the saloon chasing company and a free drink. 'My deputy will see you both.' He now turned to the lone cowboy standing by the bar with his gaze fixed upon the body. 'Name?'

There was no answer.

'Son? Son? Are you with me?'

The young cowboy's lips started to move, but his gaze remained fixed on the dead body before he stammered out, 'Jus . . . Jus . . . Justin Roy.'

'The holstered gun on your hip, is that the gun you shot this man with?'

The cowboy's body seemed to shudder as he took in a deep breath. 'I didn't mean this to happen. He's still moving a little, I seen his hand move. Are you sure he's dead?'

The sheriff ignored the confused and plaintive observation. 'Your gun? Did you use the gun I can see holstered?'

The cowboy looked up, then moved his hand instinctively to his gun, grasping the grip in response to the sheriff's request.

The onlookers, expecting him to draw, immediately reacted and stepped back as one, with some in the front row ducking their heads.

'Don't,' said the sheriff, raising his hand as the deputy brought his Winchester to the shoulder and took aim at the cowboy. The sheriff glanced back at his deputy and gave a slight nod of acknowledgement, then looked back towards the cowboy. 'Just take your hand from your gun.'

The young man lifted his hand free.

'Good. Now, is that the gun you used in the shooting?'

'Yes.' The pitch of his voice went a little higher and it was almost comical, but no one laughed.

'OK, leave it holstered and keep your hands by your sides

where I can see them. I'm going to take you into custody. My deputy and I will escort you back to the cells where you will be required to make a statement. You will be protected and fed while in detention. On the basis of your statement and the witness statements, I will determine what, if any, charges are to be laid. Do you understand?'

'Yes. I think so.'

'How old are you?

The barman went to speak for the cowboy, but the sheriff held his hand up to stop him.

The cowboy licked his lips. 'Nineteen.'

The barman raised his eyes to the ceiling.

'I'll be getting a statement from you too, Stan,' said the sheriff.

'I swear I thought they were all twenty-one,' said the barman in defence.

'What I want from you is when they came in, what they drank, then what happened before, during and immediately after the shooting.'

'Yes, Sheriff.' The barman's face showed his unease.

'Mr Osborn?'

'Yes, Sheriff,' replied the undertaker.

'Can you pronounce this man deceased? Officially?'

'The physician will need to see the body and sign the certificate, officially. But he can do that at the mortuary, as all life has expired.'

The sheriff squatted down to peer closely at the body as he examined the wound to the upper chest, which was just a little left of centre. 'I would like a photograph taken before the body is removed. Can you arrange for that?'

'It will be expensive,' said the undertaker. 'I know what Dobbs charges. It's about the same as a studio portrait.'

'We live in modern times and a photograph on paper will save me a of lot writing.' The sheriff stood up slowly. 'So, I want a picture taken before he is moved. Then, once removed I want all personal belongings collected and passed to my deputy.'

'Of course,' said the undertaker, now showing his agreement with the sheriff's demands.

'With a list.'

'Of course, all will be itemized.'

'OK, let's get this under way. Justin Roy, I am now taking you into official custody for the suspected killing of. . . .' The sheriff paused and looked at the undertaker.

The undertaker responded on cue. 'Morris Wilfred Tambling,' he said.

'Morris Wilfred Tambling,' repeated the sheriff. 'You will be required to assist in our enquiries and give a truthful account of all happenings. Do you understand?'

'Yes, sir.' The cowboy's voice was soft and compliant.

'Good.' The sheriff turned to his deputy as he rubbed two fingers against his left temple. 'Cuff him up, Jim.'

3

CHATTELS

The sheriff's head felt heavy but the headache was gone. 'Is this all of it?'

The deputy looked over the shoulder of the sheriff at the assortment of personal items in the cardboard tray. 'This is what was on him, in his pockets. Over by the counter is his belt, rifle, bedroll, saddle valise and two water canteens. His horse and saddle are being held at Spencer's and we are now paying the livery bill.'

The sheriff picked up the handgun lying in the centre of the box. It was a Colt Frontier. 'New,' he said. 'Not a mark on it.' He weighed it in his hand. 'Fine piece.' He laid it back down and picked up the pocket watch. The name Morris Wilfred Tambling was engraved upon the silver cover in fine swirled lines. 'Expensive.'

'There was over a hundred and fifty dollars in his purse,' said the deputy. 'With that sort of money I guess you can afford to drink during the working week.'

'I guess so.' The sheriff pulled up a letter from the bottom of the tray. He turned it over. It was addressed to Lawyer Derrick W. Harris, Liberty Chambers, Wood Street, Pittsburgh. The writing was neat, upright and a little large for the envelope. He slipped his thumb under the flap, then withdrew the letter. It was a single page note to the lawyer from Tambling, requesting an advance on his monthly allowance as he planned to be travelling, and would not be able to get to a bank to draw funds on the first of next month. It was dated yesterday, the day of his death. 'Has any next of kin come forward?'

'No, not yet. And—'

The sheriff looked up, waiting for the deputy to continue.

'And there is still no sign of Keap.'

'No, I suspect that we won't see him again.'

'I, I—'

The sheriff knew what was coming. It was another apology from his deputy for letting Keap disappear before he could get a statement from the dead man's travelling companion, so he stopped him by holding up the letter. 'I'll telegraph the lawyer word of the death and request him to notify the next of kin.'

The deputy looked relieved that there had been a change of conversation. 'I can do that,' he said.

'No, it's fine, Jim. You collect up all of his chattels. Ensure they are all as per the itemized list from Clem, and secure them. I'll send off the telegram.'

4

HEAVEN KNOWS

A reply telegram was received late the following afternoon. It cordially thanked the sheriff for the notification of death of Morris Wilfred Tambling and advised of the shock with which it had been received. It requested that the name of the undertaker be provided to Lawyer Derrick White Harris, so that arrangements could be made to ship the mortal remains back to Pittsburgh for burial. Then, finally, it sought details as to any charges that might have been laid against the person or persons responsible for such a terrible act.

The sheriff responded the following morning after speaking to Clement Osborne, who said he would also telegram the lawyer himself regarding the shipping of the body back East.

'Be expensive,' said the undertaker.

'I'm not too sure that cost is going to be of much concern,' said the sheriff. 'This was a cowboy with his own lawyer.'

'A well-heeled cowboy,' said the undertaker with a glint in his eye.

'Seems so,' said the sheriff. 'But why a cowboy would need a lawyer, heaven knows.'

In his telegram the sheriff advised that Justin Roy had been charged with unlawful killing and that he would go to trial in Bismarck County under a district circuit judge, who was yet to be determined by name. He also advised that a Mr James Keap, who had recently befriended Mr Tambling and had been with him at the time of his death, had absconded before a statement could be taken. *However*, he wrote in pencil upon the telegram paper,

*a notice has been posted within the State of Missouri seeking his appre-
hension and attendance at the trial.*

Lawyer Harris responded the following day, once again
thanking the sheriff for the information provided and made the
statement that in light of Mr James Keap's absence: *it would be
prudent to postpone any court proceedings until such time as he is found
and available to give evidence.*

The sheriff pressed his lips together when he read the
telegram. 'Lawyer Harris,' he then said out loud. 'That is for the
court to decide, not me and not you.'

5

FULL MARKET PRICE

The body of Morris Wilfred Tambling was shipped back to
Pittsburgh in a refrigerated rail car.

'Lord knows how much that cost?' said Clem Osborne.

The sheriff just shrugged. 'I have no idea.'

'About the same as a side of beef,' said a joker who was listening in.

The undertaker was mortified by the comment.

When the body arrived in Pittsburgh it was moved to
Arlington Avenue under the care of Bingham & Son. At their
funeral parlour the body was redressed in a bespoke navy suit
made by an English tailor on Delray Street, then laid out in a
solid mahogany casket lined with white taffeta. The head of the
deceased lay upon a silk covered pillow.

The service was conducted at the First Presbyterian Church of

Pittsburgh. The congregation was small but included some notables, mostly old men who had long retired from their professions and had come to pay their respects to the father of the deceased, Richard Standley Tambling; a tall, thin man with cold eyes and a frigid handshake.

Tambling senior did not speak at his son's funeral; that duty was left to others. The first was the preacher, a young man with a liking for theological language who lamented the loss, then referred to all the joys of Christianity and 'the welcoming we shall all receive on that day of reckoning'. The looks from the faces before him were reflective but unconvinced.

The second was Lawyer Harris who was respectful but brief.

'It's not what he said, but what he left out,' came the comment on the lawyer's eulogy from an old senator, who whispered to a banker who sat next to him. 'There was always scandal surrounding that boy and his mother. How Dick could have allowed himself such folly with a woman like that was always beyond me.'

'If you don't know by now, you never will,' came the reply.

'What do you mean?'

The conversation continued in low tones and from the corner of the mouth. 'She was half his age,' said the banker. 'And for that he paid the price in cold hard cash.'

The final speaker was Ralph Stanthorpe, who had been Morris Tambling's schoolteacher. He spoke in vague terms with emphasis upon class attendance rather than classroom performance. It seems that he was a boy who could read and write, but enjoyed the outdoors and hankered for adventure.

'He could be a spiteful little chap,' said the banker.

'I've known many spiteful men,' said the old senator. 'But is it a sin?'

'No, but the way he spent money was. He never seemed to know its worth. It all came too easy.'

The service finished on time and Morris Wilfred Tambling was laid to rest in the Tambling family plot in the Union Dale cemetery to the sounds of a muffled drum. The inscription upon the headstone, which was eventually put in place, was simple: *Unto God*, it said with the dates: 27 January 1880 to 4 April 1899.

His personal possessions, which had been marked for the attention of Lawyer Harris, were then passed on to Richard Tambling, who dismissed the engraved pocket watch with disdain, but showed a keen interest in the Colt Frontier. 'Did he have this with him when he was killed?' he asked.

'I believe so,' said the lawyer.

'Then why did he not defend himself?'

'I don't know; perhaps he tried.'

'Hmm,' said Tambling senior as he continued to examine the handgun. 'It looks unused.'

'The items included a letter from the sheriff asking for instructions as to what should be done with Morris's saddle and horse,' said the lawyer.

'Has he made an offer?'

'No, I don't believe he wishes to purchase them.'

'If he does,' responded Richard Tambling in a caustic tone, 'He will have to pay full market price.'

6

FRIGHT

The judge was just one week shy of his eightieth birthday; this would be his last circuit and therefore his last opportunity to deliver justice from the bench to the citizens of Bismarck

County. The sheriff presented him with the sheaf of legal papers bound by a red ribbon. The judge pulled upon the tie and read the cover sheet.

'Tambling, Tambling, where have I heard that name?' The judge licked the tip of his finger, then pressed it to the top corner of the page and turned, his eyes downcast as he read. 'Any word from the family of the deceased?'

'My dealings have been via telegram and through the family lawyer in Pennsylvania. The body has been returned, but I have no more information than that.'

The judge kept reading as he stroked his white beard to a point under his chin. 'When was that?'

'Two, three weeks.'

'Are they wanting to be in attendance?'

'I don't know. Do we need to wait?'

'No, I don't think we need to hold up the trial. It isn't going to bring Morris Wilfred Tambling back from the grave and you have been feeding the accused for over a month.' The judge pulled at the point of his white whiskers. 'What about young Justin Roy: any family?'

'Mother only. On a small farm, Iowa way.'

'Does he want representation?'

'Hasn't asked.'

The judge turned another page. 'What's his temperament like, Ben?'

'Remorseful and worried.'

'That's a good start.' The judge turned another page, his eyes darting over the first of the witness statements. When he got to the end he gave a small sigh, then quickly moved on to the following two statements. He nodded as he read the second.

The sheriff sat on the corner of his desk, observing but not interrupting.

The judge got to the last of the documents and saw the photograph of the body. He examined it in detail, a crumpled young man lying on his back, one leg twisted at an odd angle, a hand turned upright with fingers curled as if to hold an apple, and two open eyes staring into vacant space with a look of frozen astonishment. He turned back to the start of the papers and looked at the name Justin Roy, the accused.

'You have charged him with unlawful killing. That seems fair on the basis of what I have read. It can be upgraded if needs be.' He then looked at the cover sheet again. 'Tambling, Tambling,' he said. 'Where have I heard that name before?'

'Sound familiar?'

'Familiar yes, but from where I can't recall.' He slid the ribbon back around the papers, then looked up. 'Do we have a jury?'

'I have seven men and the three witnesses.'

'Jury of six is all we need, but keep number seven in mind until I take a look at them. What do you make of the witnesses? Reliable?'

'One is a local who spends most of his spare time in the Silver Eagle.'

'Big drinker?'

'Can't afford it. Old miner who's mostly chasing company. No trouble. Likes to have a chat.'

'Second?'

'Manager of the stock and feed store. I'm not sure if he is even a drinker. He had taken one of his customers over to the saloon. He's a no-nonsense type, would make a good mayor, but he's not interested in politics.'

'Smart man. And the third?'

'Bartender and part-owner of the Silver Eagle. He's a reluctant witness.'

'And why is that?' The judge stiffened as he spoke.

'All these boys were under age and he was serving them hard liquor.'

The judge relaxed a little. 'I see, so he doesn't have anything against the law, he just doesn't want to be implicated and have his licence revoked.'

Sheriff nodded. 'That's about it.'

'Well, that will keep him on his best behaviour when he gives evidence.'

The sheriff looked shy and rubbed his hand across his mouth. 'We did have a fourth, but he ran out on us, even before we could get a statement. His name is James Keap. He was staying in the Windsor with Tambling and had known him for about a week. They had come into the saloon together and were then joined by Roy. He was there when the shooting occurred.'

'I saw his name on the list.' The judge's voice was like gravel and showed his displeasure. 'So how come he got away?'

'He was excused to relieve himself when we were taking statements down at the Eagle. As soon as he got out the back door he was gone. He went straight to the livery, got his horse and went. Didn't even pick up up his personal belongings from the boarding-house. I put out a recall by telegram, but he's gone.'

'Not like you, Ben. You always play by the rule book. So what happened?'

The sheriff was uncomfortable and shifted his backside a little on the edge of the desk.

The judge kept his eyes fixed on the sheriff, who rubbed his mouth a second time. Then he looked over at the deputy at the front of the office, who was serving a woman at the counter.

'It was young Jim who fell for that trick, wasn't it?'

'I was still in charge,' said the sheriff, 'you can't blame him.'

The judge picked up the papers. 'We go to trial tomorrow. Can you have everyone in the community hall by eleven?'

'Eleven,' repeated the sheriff back to the judge. 'I'll have everyone there.'

'Well, not everyone.'

The corners of the sheriff's mouth pulled down with embarrassment at the dig by the judge over his missing witness.

As the judge stood up he put his hand on the lawman's shoulder. 'Don't fret yourself on this one, Ben. Some men run away from the first sign of trouble, and it doesn't necessarily make them any less courageous or any guiltier than the rest of us. When a young man sees death up close for the first time he can sometimes get the fright of his life.'

7

ALL RISE

The jury sat in a row on spindle-back chairs across to the left of a long table that had been placed at the far end of the community hall. This would be the bench at which the judge would preside over the trial. The six jurors had collectively met with the judge twenty minutes prior, in the small room at the back of the hall, where they had been questioned as to any relationship they might have had with the defendant or the deceased. None had had any contact with either man. Norm Estleman, the owner of the lumber yard, was elected to be the jury foreman. He was the shortest man of the six and the only one who wore a suit.

On the opposite side of the hall from the jury were two chairs. In one sat the accused, Justin Roy, a confused young man with his hands cuffed and eyes that darted and displayed his confusion. To his side sat the deputy, upright, with a Winchester across his lap. Before the bench was a small stand from where evidence would be given, and back from that were the neat rows of long backless pews that had been taken from the church for the occasion. These seats now became filled, to the shuffling feet of the public who had come to watch. The front row was reserved for those who would be called to give evidence and at one end, closest to the jury, sat the sheriff, who was also designated to act as the clerk of the court. On the second row sat the reporter from the *Bismarck Bulletin*, a bespectacled man in his forties who wore a waistcoat. His notebook was balanced on his knee as he looked around, counting the heads in the gallery.

The judge came to the door of the back room, stood still for a moment and adjusted his black robes, then nodded towards the sheriff who, now also standing, said, 'All rise.'

Feet shuffled and scraped before one of the pews at the back fell over with a loud thump, which was followed by some muted laughter.

The judge took his position behind and to the centre of the long table. His gavel cracked upon the small mahogany block before him, which bought about immediate silence. 'All quiet. Be seated. This court is now in session. Sheriff, please read the charge.'

The sheriff, still standing, said, 'Your Honour, I bring before you a case of unlawful killing that took place on Tuesday 4 April 1899 in the front room of the Silver Eagle Saloon, in the Precinct of Lewis, Bismarck County. On that day, at approximately four o'clock in the afternoon, Morris Wilfred Tambling, from Pennsylvania, was killed with a single shot from a .45 Colt pistol. The bullet entered the upper chest to the left in the vicinity of the heart. Death was believed to be quick.'

A woman three rows back gasped.

The sheriff turned his head to see where the sound had come from, then continued to read his declaration, which he held in his left hand. 'Before your Honour is Justin Roy, a male citizen of Iowa, aged nineteen years, who had come to Bismarck County to seek employment. He was present at the shooting and has made a statement confirming that it was he who fired the shot.'

'May the accused rise,' said the judge.

Justin Roy looked surprised and confused and remained seated. The deputy stood and placed his hand under Roy's elbow to motion him to stand.

'How do you plead to the charge of unlawful killing?'

'I, I didn't mean to—'

The deputy leant in close to the accused and whispered into his ear.

'Not guilty,' said Roy who went to sit, but the deputy kept a hand under his arm and whispered again. Justin Roy nodded on receiving the prompt, then said. 'Not guilty, your Honour.'

'Is any one acting on behalf of the defendant?'

'No, your Honour,' said the sheriff. 'He has chosen to seek the mercy of the court.'

'May it be made known to all those who are in this court and especially the jury, that when the sheriff appraised me of this young man's decision to defend himself, I sent instructions via the sheriff for him to reconsider his position. Was that done, Sheriff?'

'It was.'

'Yet he still wished to defend himself?'

'He did, your Honour.'

The judge looked over at the accused, who sat nodding his head.

'OK,' said the judge. 'I believe he has made a statement, a written and signed statement.'

'He has,' said the sheriff.

'Sheriff, please present his statement to the court.'

The sheriff moved forward and handed a single sheet of paper to the judge, who held it aloft to show the public and jury before saying. 'I have that statement and it will be presented as evidence to the jury.'

The sheriff returned to his pew and sat.

'I accept his decision,' said the judge, who then turned to the jury. 'However, if I believe that it is in the interests of the defendant to have legal representation, I will stall this hearing until such time as that can be arranged. Does the jury understand?'

The jury nodded back to the judge as one.

The judge turned to the accused. 'You may sit.'

The deputy put his hand on the young man's shoulder to

motion for him to sit.

'Call the first witness,' said the judge.

8

I DO

'I do,' said the first witness, who stood directly before the judge, after he had been administered the oath.

'Now standing before this court, I would like you to tell in your own words what you saw and heard in regard to the killing of Morris Tambling.'

'He did it,' came the shriek of the old miner. 'I was there and I saw him do it.'

The public burst into laughter. The judged whacked the gavel upon the block three times and looked stern.

The crowd hushed.

'Just go through what you saw prior to the shooting. Start before the deadly shot was fired.'

'All right then, I'll do that.' The witness scratched at the side of his unshaven face. 'Before the shot was fired,' he mumbled to himself, 'I came into the Eagle and saw him,' he pointed to the accused, 'drinking with two other young'uns. They was near the corner of the bar, holding it up. Then some voices were raised and Stan,' he pointed to the barman of the Silver Eagle, who was sitting on the front pew waiting to give evidence, 'told them to hush up. Which they did for a while, then that one got agitated and pulled his gun. It was a lightning draw, I can tell ye. I've seen some fast ones from the old days, but this boy was fast and straight. That pistol came out of the holster like grease.' The witness whipped his hand up from his side as if drawing a handgun, his finger sticking out and pointing towards the jury. 'The shot fired. Lordy, what a racket! Near dropped me drink.'

Some soft laughter was heard from the public gallery.

The judge gave a solemn look and the noise stopped.

'Got him high.' The witness clenched his chest. 'He staggered back. "You got me", he said. "You got me good this time".' The witness bent at his knees and stepped back out of the small witness stand, tottering as he went. 'He fell to the floor, a dying man. And he bit the dust.' The witness dropped his head.

Some members of the gallery began to clap.

The judge's gavel banged hard. 'Quiet,' he said with command. Then he asked, 'Any questions?'

The sheriff shook his head as he stood. 'No, your Honour.'

The accused was prompted by the deputy to respond. 'No, no your Honour.'

The judged looked relieved. 'Next witness.'

Stan Lynch, the barman from the Silver Eagle, was directed to the stand to take the oath.

'When they came in I swear to God I thought they were all over twenty-one.' So began his evidence.

'I bet you did,' mumbled the judge. 'Just get to the point in question.'

'The one that was shot, Tambling, he was drinking hard, mostly whiskey, but they all started on beer. The other two, the one that did the runner and the shooter, stayed on beer. They were OK. It was Tambling who started to become loathsome. I was just about ready to ask him to leave when the argument commenced.'

'Is that so,' mumbled the judge to himself.

'When the shooting started I was at the other end of the bar serving. Scared the hell out of me. I turned to see what had happened, but by then Tambling was out of view. He had fallen to the floor and was obscured by the bar. The man, Roy, Justin Roy, was standing there with his pistol drawn and looking down at the floor. He then put the pistol back in his holster, real casual like. Some of the patrons came to the aid of the wounded man, but he was pronounced dead. You could of bowled me over when I found out all three were under age.'

'Anything else?' asked the judge.

'Only that they looked much older.'

The judge cut him short and looked over at the sheriff. 'Any questions?'

'No, your Honour.'

The judge turned to the defendant. 'Any questions?'

Roy stood up quickly. 'No, your Honour.' He sat down just as quickly.

The bartender turned to resume his seat.

'Don't move,' said the judge, 'I have a question.'

Stan Lynch froze and the blood seemed to drain from his face. 'Yes,' he said slowly.

'The first witness said their voices were raised and you told them to hush up, which they did for a while. Is that correct?'

The barman looked relieved. 'Yes, that is correct.'

'So if you were about ready to ask Morris Tambling to leave, why didn't you do it then?'

The blood had just started to return to the barman's face. It now drained away again. 'I . . . I . . . well, I really don't know.'

'Nor do I, Mister Bartender, nor do I.'

The barman looked like a fish thrown upon a muddy river-bank, with a mouth that opened and closed, but from which no noise emanated.

'Next witness,' said the judge, to the relief of the barman, who now resumed his seat to mop his perspiring brow.

'Name?'

'Harry Burrell, and I swear to tell the truth.'

'Go on,' said the judge.

'I entered the saloon some ten minutes before the shooting with Mr Desmond Moulton, manager of the Tall T. He had just ordered five wagonloads of sawn lumber and as it was too late for him to return to the T that evening, he decided to say in town. I offered to buy him a drink and he accepted the offer.' The witness stood straight-backed and did not move within the confines of the small stand. His hands were in front of his body about waist height and he gestured a little as he spoke. His voice was clear and measured. 'The three young men at the other end of the bar came to our notice when voices were raised. The barman spoke to them and they quietened down.' The witness adjusted his stance, showing that he was a little more relaxed in giving evidence. 'Mr Moulton excused himself and left through the back to go to the outhouse. During this time I stood at the bar and observed the three young men. I had nothing else to do, as I am not a drinker and had only chilled tonic water. The man I now know to be Mr Tambling leant over and seemed to say something to Mr Roy. I don't know what was said but Mr Roy became agitated.'

The judge interrupted. 'Agitated?'

'Yes. He became upset and seemed to be asking for a retraction. I am not sure, but I think he said: "You take that back or by God you will pay".' The witness adjusted his stance again. 'Mr Tambling responded by spitting at Mr Roy.'

'Spitting?' said the judge. 'Spitting?'

'Yes, your Honour.'

The judge searched through some of the papers before him, then said. 'In your witness statement you used the term "spat" did you not?'

'I did?'

'Were you referring to a spat as in an argument or quarrel?'

'No your Honour. Mr Roy was physically spat upon by Mr Tambling.'

'I see. And with that Mr Roy then shot Mr Tambling?'

'No.'

'No?'

The public gallery responded with instant chatter.

'Quiet.' The judge's gavel banged with two quick blows.

'I have given this much thought, Your Honour, and I have come to the conclusion that Mr Tambling deliberately spat in Mr Roy's face in order to distract him while he tried to draw his revolver from his holster.'

The gallery instantly returned to chatter.

The gavel struck thee times in quick succession. 'Quiet.'

The decorum of the courtroom returned.

'Are you sure?'

'As sure as I can be, Your Honour. I have deliberately gone back over my thoughts since witnessing the events and believe it to be so.'

'And you say you don't drink alcohol?'

'That is correct.'

'So you were stone-cold sober during your observations?'

'Yes.'

'And you have not had a drop to drink since making those observations?'

'No, Your Honour.'

'And you believe your reflections are true and accurate?'

'I do.'

'Are you connected to the accused in any way? A relative? A friend? A business associate?'

'No, Your Honour. I have never met the accused.'

'I see,' said the judge, who wrote a note upon the papers before him. 'Thank you, that will be all.'

9

JUST SAY YES

After a lunch of boiled chicken that had the taste of moist straw, the judge reconvened the court at 2 p.m. sharp.

'Now young man, I want you to take your time and tell the court in your own words what happened from the time you met Morris Tambling in the Silver Eagle Saloon to the time the shot was fired and the sheriff arrived.'

'Do I start now?' asked Roy.

'Yes, you start now.'

'I'd been drinking. I don't normally drink. It went to my head. I don't want to drink no more.'

The words babbled out of the young cowboy like a brook after the spring sun has melted the snow. The judge stopped him.

'I understand that, and your repentance is noted, but what I, what this court, and what the jury want, is to hear about the events. How it happened, truthfully and plain and simple.'

The cowboy nodded. 'I met Morrie—' He stopped, then corrected himself. 'I met Morris Tambling for the first time in the Silver Eagle.' He stopped and looked up at the ceiling for a second or two. 'I actually met Jim Keap first. I went into the saloon to ask around for work, but had no luck and Jim said hello. He seemed like a good fellow, so I said howdy back and got talking. He introduced me to Morrie—' He corrected himself again, 'Morris, who seemed OK, at first, but then he began to drink too much and talk too much. After a while he started to annoy me and I knew I should have left, but Jim was OK and he was giving me pointers, where I might find some work and what I should look out for. Then Morris started to say things about Iowa and that got me riled a bit. So I told him to put a cork in it.'

The judge intervened. 'Was that the reason for voices being raised?'

'Yes sir, it was.'

'What sort of things was he saying against Iowa?'

'That it was a backward state and that everybody that came from there was backward.'

'Was it done in jest? A joke?'

'No sir. If he had been jesting I would have played along and jested back, but his was no banter. He was serious and rude.'

'Rude enough—' The judge stopped and turned to the sheriff. 'I think it would be in the interests of this court if you questioned the defendant on the detail, Sheriff. Can you do that?'

The sheriff stood. 'Yes, Your Honour.' He rubbed two fingers against his left temple, then took up the questioning. 'Was Morris Tambling rude enough for you to want to kill him?'

'No sir, not then. I didn't like what he was saying over Iowa, but that's not enough to warrant killing a man.'

'So, what was it that riled you?'

'He got personal.'

'How personal?'

'He started attacking my parents. He said my father must have been a jackass for me to be so hick.'

'What did you say?'

'I offered to fight him, outside.'

'Gunfight?'

'No sir. Fistfight.'

'But you didn't?'

'No sir. Jim said let him be, that he got like that when he had a skinful. Mean like. He said let it go and he will eventually go and sleep it off.'

'Then what happened?'

'I said I was going, and just as I was deciding, he leant over and said something about my mother.'

'Then what happened?'

'I got upset, real upset. He had pushed me too far.'

'Then what happened?'

'I shot him. I didn't mean to but—'

'Sheriff,' said the judge.

The sheriff nodded. He knew what the judge wanted. 'Just back up a little. Explain exactly what happened in regard to the shooting.'

The defendant looked a little confused. 'Well, I drew and I fired.'

The judge looked back at the sheriff.

'This is important,' said the sheriff. 'Did you draw first or did Tambling try to draw first?'

The defendant looked even more confused. 'I rightly don't know. It all happened real quick like. I have tried to remember, but I can't be sure. You see, I don't recall drawing my gun or pulling the trigger. All I remember is looking down at my hand after the gun had gone off.'

'You heard what the third witness said. Is he correct? Were you spat upon?'

The court was hushed.

The defendant was slowly shaking his head and looking down at the floor.

The sheriff was leaning forward staring at the young cowboy as a voice in his head yelled, 'Just say yes, just say yes.'

The cowboy kept shaking his head slowly. 'I guess—' Then he looked up at the sheriff and said, 'I truthfully cannot recall.'

10

STRAIGHT AND TRUE

The judge's instructions to the jury were brief and simple. 'You must make a determination if the killing was justified, and you must do that on the evidence put before you, and that evidence alone. You have heard from three witnesses who have each recounted what they saw, but no one account is able to provide a complete rendering of events; that is not unusual.' As the judge spoke he stroked the whiskers beneath his chin. 'Until that fatal shot was fired this was an everyday occasion that deserved no more than casual observance from those who were there at that time. In fact, many of the patrons of the Silver Eagle paid no heed until the shot was fired. However, it is on the evidence, complete or otherwise, that you must now decide, and when you do, you must do so on your own conscience and your own conscience alone. You must not do so under any duress.' The judged noticed that a brow creased on the forehead of one of the jurors. 'You must not be persuaded by another member of the jury,' he explained. 'It must be your decision and yours alone.'

The confused juror seemed enlightened and was nodding his head in solemn agreement.

'This court will now adjourn while we await your decision and you should take as long as necessary, as this is a serious matter and deserves your full consideration.'

The responsibility showed on all six faces and that was exactly what the judge wanted to see.

The sheriff escorted the six men across the street to a top floor room at the Orange Tree boarding house, while the deputy returned the accused man to the cell. He then came across to the boarding house to relieve the sheriff and take up a vigil on a stool just outside the closed door.

When the sheriff returned to his office the young cowboy called from the cell for a cup of water. The sheriff brought it to him and Justin Roy asked what he thought the jury's decision would be.

What surprised the sheriff was that he felt an urge to console the cowboy in his plight. As a lawman for more than sixteen years he had hardened towards those who broke the law, then did their best to lie their way out of justice, which often included a good dose of false remorse. But the demeanour of this boy and his answers, along with Harry's evidence, showed Justin Roy to be a trustworthy, if naive young man. However, the sheriff still knew that an acquittal would be difficult. Harry was just one witness, and one witness alone. Had the young cowboy said, under oath, that he had only gone for his gun to defend himself, then it would have carried some weight in the minds of the jury. Over the years the sheriff had seen some appalling verdicts and he feared this might prove to be another such occasion.

'It is in the hands of the jury,' he said and saw the look of desperation on the young man's face. So he added, 'You spoke straight and true and that deserves recognition.'

Justin Roy seemed to be lightened by the sheriff's words and showed some cheer on his face. 'I told only what I knew to be true, as I swore to do.' he said.

The sheriff nodded in agreement. 'I know you did, and it was commendable.'

11

WRITE IT DOWN

The jury shuffled back into the community hall and the judge reconvened the court with a crack of the gavel. The sharp sound of authority displayed the judge's serious intent and the onlookers stopped talking and shuffling, to now sit in earnest, as if attending a funeral service. Their looks reflected the seriousness of the affair, with some of the women showing apprehension at what the judgment might be.

Most had expected a verdict from the jury within an hour or two, or maybe three, but certainly no more. That deliberation had continued for one night and one half-day, behind a locked door in the Orange Tree boarding house, had been a talking matter for all. The judge had sent a note to the foreman after breakfast, to see if further instructions were required that might assist the jury to make a determination. The note returned to the judge simply read, *No thanks, Judge.*

The sheriff looked hard at each juror's face as he tried to read their minds. Had they found Justin Roy guilty of unlawful killing or not? He glanced again back over the six faces, searching, trying to catch a sign or a glimpse of their intentions, but he could make nothing of it. He, like all of the others in that hall, had no idea as to what was to come.

'Jury,' said the judge. 'What verdict have you come to regarding the charge of the unlawful killing of Morris Wilfred Tambling of Pennsylvania by Mr Justin Roy of Iowa. Do you find him guilty or not guilty?'

The jury foreman slowly stood then rubbed his splayed fingers down his trouser legs before clasping his hands under his chin as if to pray. 'Your Honour,' he said, his voice wavering slightly. 'We're hung.'

A thump to the floor, followed by the clatter of an upturned chair upon the boards, brought those in the public gallery to their feet to see what had happened. The judge stood too, as the deputy sheriff leant forward over the slumped body of the defendant.

'What happened?' asked the judge.

'I don't know,' said the deputy. 'He seems to have dropped into a dead faint.'

'Smelling salts,' said the sheriff, turning towards the standing congregation. 'Do any of the ladies here have aromatic spirits with them?'

'I have some,' came a reply from a woman dressed in green. She made her way towards the sheriff while pulling on the drawstrings of her reticule. She handed a small blue bottle to the sheriff, who then walked briskly over to his deputy, who was crouched over Justin Roy. The sheriff removed the tiny glass stopper and waved the bottle under the nose of the unconscious man.

'Maybe a little closer,' suggested the deputy.

The young cowboy gave a brief spluttering cough as the ammonia woke him from his faint.

The sheriff and deputy helped him back on to his chair with a hand under each arm. The sheriff then asked if he was OK.

The cowboy nodded his head, then wiped his nose.

The sheriff leant in close to hear what he had to say, but none of the onlookers could hear what was said.

'What was the cause of his faint?' asked the judge.

Justin Roy still looked a little dazed, his hands gripping at the arms of his chair. He nodded again to the sheriff, who turned and approached the judge, then leant forward so that he could speak quietly.

'He thought the jury said he was going to be hung.'

'Oh,' said the judge, 'I see. Now that would be quite a shock to anyone. Did you explain?'

'Yes, but I think you may need to clarify as well.'

The judged nodded as the sheriff stepped back and the gavel cracked upon the small mahogany block.

'The court will proceed.' He turned towards the jury. 'Mister Foreman, as I understand it, you are tied in a vote of three apiece.' The judge then turned his head slightly towards the defendant. 'Or what we refer to as a hung decision.' He turned his head back towards the jury. 'Is that correct?'

'It is, Your Honour.'

'Are you seeking clarification on any point of evidence that was put before you, which might result in a solution to this impasse?'

'We believe so, Your Honour.'

'And what would that be in particular?'

The foreman turned and glanced at his fellow jurors before he spoke, as if to receive a silent confirmation. 'In the evidence provided, we heard that the defendant was spat upon.' The foreman paused. 'That is correct, isn't it?'

'Yes it is,' confirmed the judge.

'And that this may have been done to distract the defendant so that—' The foreman turned his head towards the other jurors for instruction and received a mumbled word. 'So that the spitter could draw his gun first.'

'That is correct,' said the judge.

'Did anyone else witness the spitting, Your Honour?'

The judge looked a little confused.

The sheriff looked annoyed and wondered why it mattered.

'I seen it too,' came the call. It was the first witness, the old miner, in his shrieking voice, but this time there was no smirking or laughter from the gallery. Instead some stood – those at the back – looking to see from whom the voice had come, on the front pew. 'I seen him spat at,' continued the call.

'Thank you,' said the judge to the witness, then he addressed the jury foreman. 'Yes, it was observed by a second witness, but that will need to be recorded under oath for you to consider it in your determination.' The judge made a note. 'Why do you see that as significant?'

The responsibility upon the foreman seemed to weigh down on him as if it were a physical weight upon his hunched shoulders. 'We believe the events leading up to the shooting are important, not just the shooting alone.'

'I agree,' said the judge. 'The reasons for violent actions are often explained or even justified, when known.'

The foreman seemed to gain confidence from the judge's comment. 'We believe so as well, Your Honour.'

The other jury members nodded in agreement.

'Prior to being spat upon, the man killed, Mr Tambling, was observed to lean across and say something to Mr Roy.'

'That is correct,' said the judge. 'That evidence was given under oath and recorded.'

The sheriff leant forward a little to hear. He didn't know where this was going, but he sensed the jury was striving to find the truth and deliver an honest verdict.

'Mr Roy then asked Mr Tambling to withdraw what was said. That is correct, isn't it?'

The judge looked down at his papers as if to check his facts before giving his response. 'Yes,' he said. 'That is correct.'

'But he didn't, did he? Instead, he spat in Mr Roy's face.'

'Yes, that is correct,' repeated the judge.

'Then,' said the jury foreman, 'what we, the jury, would like to know, Your Honour, is what was said to Mr Roy.'

The judge pushed his lips forward, as if to pucker for a kiss, then nodded in agreement to the request. 'Let the court put that question to the defendant, who is still under oath.'

The deputy put his hand under the arm of the cowboy to help him stand.

'Would you tell the court what was said?' asked the judge.

The young man's face looked pasty. 'I would prefer not,' came his response.

'And why is that?' asked the judge.

The accused licked his lips and looked around at the gallery before dropping his head. 'It contains an impolite word, Your Honour. One that should never be said in the company of ladies.'

'I see.' The judge looked across at the sheriff then motioned for him to come across to the table. 'Can you read and write, Mr Roy? Because if you cannot I will get the sheriff to do it for you.' The judge handed the sheriff a small piece of paper and a short pencil.

'I can both read and write.'

'Good. I want you to write it down, clearly, what was said.'

'It was just one word, Your Honour.'

'OK. Just write down the one word.'

The deputy placed the flat side of his Winchester butt upon the leg of the cowboy, who leant forward and wrote upon the paper, then handed it back to the sheriff.

The sheriff folded the paper in half and carried it to the judge, who unfolded it, read it, refolded it and handed it back to the sheriff. He motioned for Ireland to show it to the jury.

Just as the sheriff was about to hand it to the foreman, the judge spoke. 'Before the jury sees what is written, could the accused tell us whom Mr Tambling was referring to when he used such a foul term?'

The cowboy stood up and seemed to have trouble getting the words out, but the judge was patient.

'My, my' – he glanced around the court – 'my mother.'

'I see,' said the judge. 'Sheriff, please show the jury what is written.'

The sheriff handed the note to the foreman, who read it and seemed a little shocked. He folded it, shaking his head and passed it to the next juror. Each of them read and shook his head in condemnation of the foul term used against the cowboy's mother.

The gallery eagerly watched the proceedings and could only guess at what was written.

'Are there any more questions?' asked the judge.

The foreman turned to his fellow jurors, who shook their heads. 'No, Your Honour.'

'Then will this help you in your decision?'

'I believe it will,' said the foreman.

'So, the sheriff will escort you back—'

The jury foreman interrupted the judge. 'I don't believe that will be necessary, Your Honour.' He turned to the other five in the jury, who all nodded in agreement. 'We the jury,' said Norm Estleman, drawing himself up to his full height of no more than five foot five and half inches, 'Find the accused not guilty of unlawful killing.'

12

UNFINISHED BUSINESS

The news of the acquittal of Justin Roy of Iowa reached Richard Standley Tambling the following week. His fury at the decision surprised many, as he had expressed little emotion on hearing of the death of his only son, Morris, the previous month. Even during the funeral service he had shown little reaction, sitting frozen and rigid, looking straight ahead, which the other mourners incorrectly interpreted as an expression of dignified and stoic sorrow.

His butler, however, a tall man of few words, who had been in the employ of the Tambling family for nearly thirty years, was the only one who had any sense of what was going on. He knew that Richard Tambling was a man who could hate in a rage without end. Even the most mean of men would eventually tire of the unrelenting endeavour required to hate for so long, but not Richard Tambling.

He was a man of fortitude when it came to vengeance, especially when something was taken from him. It mattered not how small, inconsequential, or worthless that item might be, and Morris Tambling had been declared, on more than one occasion by his father, to be insignificant and useless. But Morris was still a Tambling in name, albeit from a gold digger who had tried unsuccessfully to sink her claws into the fortune that had come from the once great Tambling Steel Company of Pennsylvania.

'Hicks,' he bellowed. 'Rural hicks with no sense of worth or decency. What else could be expected from such stupid country fools?'

'Yes, sir,' said the butler.

'What do they know of justice? Nothing.'

'Yes, sir.'

'They allow a boy to be shot down and then acquit the man who did it. Where is the justice of a life for a life? Tell me that? Don't they read the Bible west of the Mississippi?'

'I don't know, sir.'

'So if the hicks won't give me justice, I will get it myself.'

'You will, sir?' The butler tried to hide his look of astonishment.

'Yes, I will, and it will be the sort of justice that they will understand. Strong and straight justice that requires no façade of a bucolic court of law.'

The butler stood perfectly still trying not to draw attention to himself as he watched the tirade.

'Get me Harris.'

'Your lawyer, sir?' said the butler in a measured tone.

'Yes, of course my lawyer. I want to see Harris straight away. I have unfinished business of law to attend to.'

13

PLAY IT SAFE

'You don't have to leave.'

The young cowboy pulled the strap tight around his bedroll, then looked up at the sheriff. 'I think it's for the best. I had planned to find work here and then drift south, even down to Texas, but after all that has happened I think it best that I return home. I . . . I sort of miss it. Miss it a real lot, just of late.'

'I can understand that,' said the sheriff. 'So where is home exactly?'

'Red Oak. Red Oak, Iowa.'

'You born there?'

The cowboy nodded as he buckled the strap, then patted his hand upon the bedroll.

'And how are you planning to get there?'

'The same way I came down, but opposite. Hamilton, Gallatin, Bethany, Bedford and then Red Oak.'

'What's that then? A hundred and fifty – sixty miles? A good ride.'

'Guess. But I'm in no hurry, I've only got one horse, so I'm going take my time. If I take a week or more it's of little matter, as long as I am heading home.' The cowboy secured the bedroll to the back of the saddle above the two bulky brown canvas valises. 'Besides, I think this will be the last time I go wandering. Too dangerous.'

The sheriff smiled at the humour of the young cowboy. 'Well, you ride easy back to Iowa.'

'I will.'

'And take care.'

'Do that too.'

The sheriff went to speak then stopped, turned to go, stopped again, then turned back once more. 'The other fella that was with you? The one who skedaddled?'

'Jim Keap.'

'Yes. Was he close to Tambling? Friends?'

'They were friends, but I don't think they were real close. Why?'

The sheriff hesitated before he spoke, pressing his lips together. 'You be careful.'

The cowboy squinted. 'Sure,' he said slowly. 'You think Jim Keap might want to settle up?'

'I can't answer that, but it did cross my mind.'

The cowboy shook his head. 'I don't think Jim wants anything to do with what happened. Besides, I was found not guilty, fair and square, in a court of law.'

'Yes I know.' The sheriff extended his hand.

The cowboy's grip was loose and showed that he was ill at ease.

'I'm sure all will be OK,' said the sheriff trying to lighten his tone. 'When you get older, like me, you always tend to want to play it safe.'

The cowboy pulled himself into the saddle. 'And that's what I intend to do, play it safe.'

'Good man,' said the sheriff, lifting his hand in a wave. The cowboy waved back, then flicked the reins and clicked his tongue for his mount to break into a canter.

'Good advice,' said the deputy, standing behind the sheriff.

The words took the sheriff by surprise. 'What was that?'

'Your advice, to watch out.'

'I think all I did was to put the wind up him.'

'That's not a bad thing. I just don't think he understands that he now has to live with any consequences that come from killing a man.'

'No, I don't think he understands either. But hopefully he'll be safe and sound in Red Oak, Iowa.'

'Hopefully,' repeated the deputy, but he didn't say it with any confidence.

14

WITH BLOOD

'If you want my opinion, Richard, I'd say leave this well alone.'

'Is that a legal opinion?' The eyes of the old man were cold upon the lawyer.

'It is both a legal opinion and that of a long-standing friend. You cannot bring Morris back and the court records show that he was killed in an armed altercation with another young man, in which he was the provocateur. That is why the court found the assailant not guilty of unlawful killing.'

'A court of country hicks.'

'Hicks or not, they followed the law of the land. I appreciate the loss you must feel, but pursuing a retrial, seeking a different outcome, a verdict of guilt, is not just expensive and doomed to failure, but it is also not good for your soul.'

'You are my attorney and I pay you for your legal opinion, not for your pastoral counselling.'

'I give it freely and as friend, Richard.' The discomfort being felt by the lawyer was now showing on his face. He had known Richard Tambling for over twenty years as a client of his law firm and, from time to time, he had admired him for his fortitude and single-mindedness. Tambling had been spectacularly successful in business, a man of determination, but also of stubborn resistance. The lawyer had on occasion believed that a bond of friendship had developed between the two men, but the reality was different. As he stared into the cold, vengeful eyes of Richard Tambling there seemed to be a vast distance between the two men that was as wide as a canyon, and his apprehension turned to alarm.

'I didn't ask you for your personal opinion and I'm paying for a legal solution to get justice for the death of my heir.'

The lawyer frowned, his eyes quizzing. 'Was he to be your heir? He is not listed in your will as a beneficiary of your estate.'

The tall gaunt figure dismissed the question.

'I want that killer to pay.'

'How, Richard? How do you want him to pay?'

'As written in the Old Testament, the law of God.' The words spat from the old man's lips. 'An eye for an eye.'

'That is foolish talk.' The lawyer was now becoming fearful.

'Foolish? You don't understand and you never will. You are a man of no ambition.'

'My ambitions have always been—' the lawyer looked crushed as he cut his words short, then said, 'I have always been your loyal servant.'

Tambling scorned the lawyer's defence without comment. 'I want you to draw up a proclamation offering a reward, on the head of the man who killed my son.'

'On what legal grounds?'

'I am not interested in the legal grounds, I'm interested in justice.'

'And how much do you propose this reward should be?'

Tambling pressed his lips together in a thin cold smile. 'Ten thousand dollars.'

'Good God, Richard, that's a king's ransom. Are you sure you know what you are doing?'

'I know precisely what I am doing. I'm paying for men of courage and might to do justice on my behalf, and I plan to pay them well.'

'That's not what you are doing. You are paying bounty to anyone who will search, find and apprehend a man who has been found innocent of the charge brought against him in a court of law. There is no legal precedence for your actions. And what then, after you apprehend him? He cannot be tried again unless there is new and compelling evidence.'

'Who said anything about apprehending? You asked how I want this man to pay for taking the life of my only son? Well, I will tell you. I want him to pay with blood. I want this man dead.'

15

A NOBLE CAUSE

'So, just how did you get my name, again?'

'I made application to the US Marshal's office and asked for a recommendation. I said that I would need to find a man of experience, skill, honesty and determination. You were recommended.'

'Really?' The large man grinned at the lawyer. 'Determination, ah.' He laughed. 'De-ter-min-ation. And just who is this Tambling?'

'A very wealthy man.'

'I can see that by the amount of money he is throwing around.'

The lawyer Harris was hesitant. 'He made his wealth in steel as a young man some forty years ago. Tambling steel has been laid down as tracks by half a dozen of the biggest railway companies of this nation. Tambling Pennsylvania would deliver high quality rails on time and at the right price. He worked hard, took risks and was rewarded well, gaining some standing within the business community, although he was a man who kept to himself. Then, twenty years ago, a young woman came into his life, they married and had an only son.'

'I get it now. The father is avenging the death of his one and only boy, so that's why he is tossing his cash around.'

'Marshal, it's not that simple.'

'It's not marshal any more,' said the solid man who sat before the lawyer, in a chair that seemed too small for his size. 'I've left all that behind, I'm . . .' He was searching for the word. He smiled. 'I'm an irregular now.'

'Irregular? Is that a title?'

'You want a title? You could call me a private investigator, a little like one of those Pinks.'

'Pinks?'

'Pinkertons. The detective agency. You know, "we never sleep", but maybe I'm not as refined; they all dress like bankers nowdays anyway, so why don't you just call me Walt?'

The lawyer paused for a moment, as if to weigh up a proposition. 'Very good,' he said, then pronounced the name in full, 'Walter', before he leant in a little closer and lowered his voice. 'As I was saying, this is not as simple as just a father seeking justice or even revenge, and I think you need to know what is involved, because it has to be treated with delicacy.'

Walt also leant forward and lowered his voice. 'Fire away, I'm all ears for any of the gossip.'

The lawyer pulled a face of concern, then leant back a little, surprised at the comment.

Walt realized that he had said the wrong thing. 'Forgive my colloquial turn of phrase. It comes from too much time in the saddle and in camps with the uncouth and uneducated.'

'I see,' said the lawyer slowly; he pondered for a moment. 'But I dare say such a life has its own excitement.'

'It sure has, but please go on. You said this was delicate.'

'The marriage did not last long; you see, another man was involved.'

'Ah, so he threw her and the youngster out?'

The lawyer pulled back again, looking offended. 'No.'

Walt bit at his tongue, but not too hard; it was far too late in life to overcome his habit of indiscretion. 'Forgive me,' he said. 'Do go on.'

'Mr Tambling did not find out for sometime about the philandering, and when it did become apparent, well it turned out that there might well have been more than one man.'

'A parlour girl, ah?'

'I wouldn't have put it like that, but yes, she had gained a reputation. But by the time he became aware of this it was all too late and she had been interned in an institution.'

'What sort of institution?' Walt had to keep the amusement from his voice because he was clearly enjoying this rare insight into a scandal involving the rich.

'A mental institution, one for the insane.'

'A place of care,' said Walt, trying hard to sound sympathetic.

The lawyer nodded in agreement. 'However, it was not before she had exhausted a great deal of money. She had unlimited access to funds and spent it on the luxuries of life, mostly furnishing, fabrics and art, all from France. Then there was the French perfume and the French champagne.'

Walter slapped his thigh. 'By God, I've tried that stuff and boy, is it good! Got as diddled as a squat.' The big man was now laughing out loud. Then through watery eyes he saw that once again his social decorum had failed him. He coughed, bringing his large hand to his mouth in a fist. 'Please, please go on.'

'A son, by the name of Morris Wilfred Tambling, was brought up in the house with a live-in nanny, and at first he seemed to be a good, sound boy. I remember when he was, oh . . .' the lawyer outstretched his hand just above the arm of the chair, 'that high,' he said. 'But as time went on it became apparent that father and son had nothing in common, nothing at all.' The lawyer pulled his chair in a little. 'Mr Tambling came to the conclusion that the boy was not of his kind . . . you know . . . his blood. He had always had his suspicions after he found out about his wife's first affair and of her past. He consulted physicians in order to find out, and while they were unable either to confirm or deny the lineage of the boy, they all agreed that there was doubt. Some of his looks and characteristics were of his mother, but not of his father.'

Walt went to speak, but bit at his tongue instead. What he was going to say would have surely offended.

'The result was a distancing in their relationship.'

Walt nodded and tried to show a face that was fitting of sympathy at the breakdown of the bond between a father and his son.

'Alas,' said the lawyer, 'They parted without warmth or sorrow, but he did provide him with an allowance. Not handsome, but still a regular allowance paid each month into his bank account.'

'So what was his boy doing down in Missouri?'

'I fear he was rambling.'

'Oh, rambling?' Walt always thought that rambling was something old men did, like himself. Young ones, he guessed, like Tambling, would have been sowing their wild oats and spending up on their allowance in every brothel and saloon that they could find. Well, at least that's what Walt would have been doing, had the circumstances been the same for him.

The two men sat in silence, the lawyer in contemplation of what might have been; while the old ex-US marshal, now an irregular, as he had called himself, thought of his own once joyous days some thirty-five years ago as a twenty-year-old, sowing *his* seed.

Walt had to stop from chuckling, so he coughed.

The lawyer came back from his solitary thoughts to ask, 'Yes?'

'You will have to enlighten me,' said Walt. 'Why is Tambling—' He corrected himself '—Mr Tambling now throwing around his money to avenge the death of a boy whom he didn't get on with and who might not have been his kin?'

'It makes no sense, does it?' The lawyer still had a faraway look in his eyes.

'Nope, it does not.'

'Mr Tambling is a proud man with a reputation. He made his fortune through his strength of character and I believe he wants to retain that reputation.'

Horseshit, thought Walt, but he nodded in agreement. 'So what is it you want from me precisely?'

'I want you to save the man who is going to be chased down and killed once this proclamation for a reward of ten thousand dollars is published.'

Walt couldn't help himself. 'Why, for hell's sake? I thought you were Tambling's attorney at law? Aren't you suppose to carry out his directions?'

'Yes, but it would be remiss of me if I let Mr Tambling go to his grave with this deed upon his conscience.'

Walt was confused. 'His conscience? If he's posting a reward for ten thousand, I'd expect he'd made up his mind on what he was doing and thrown his conscience to the wind.'

'But it will eventually come to pass with regret. It always does. That is why I cannot let this happen, so I am quietly intervening on his behalf, for sometime in the future, when he will be able to reflect and agree that this act of his was not right.' The lawyer leant forward again and grasped Walt's right hand in both of his. 'He must not know, at least not for now, what I . . . we . . . are doing.' His grip squeezed Walt's hand. 'You must find and save this young man.'

Walt felt uneasy and wanted to extract his hand from its smothering. 'I . . . I . . . I really don't know.' He rubbed his chin with his free hand, his unease showing on his face. 'How much are you willing to pay for me to do this?'

'If successful, the same price as the reward, ten thousand dollars.'

Walt gave a low, quiet whistle as he felt a sensation of emotion wash over him from his head to his toes. It was a warm surge that he hadn't felt in years. It was a wave of delightful pleasure such as comes with the scent of success, much like when a woman says yes, or when a croupier says: *collect your winnings, sir.* 'I really don't know . . .' said Walt, as he bought his free hand down from his chin to grip the two hands of the lawyer. 'I really don't know if you could have chosen a better man for this most noble of causes, because I am that man.'

The look on the lawyer's face was one of immense relief. 'I knew you were that man, Walter, I knew you were as soon as I saw you.'

However, the man sitting before the lawyer was not the man who had been recommended by the Western District of the Pennsylvania Office of the US Marshal Service – that man had the same surname and the same initials but that was all. His full name was Wallace David Garfield and he was a very different man from Walter Douglas Garfield. Wallace was terse, ambitious and upright, while Walt was genial, unambitious and at times lax. So what had happened?

The clerk had replaced a slip of paper folded within the letter signed by Marshal Frederick C. Leonard, giving the address for Wallace, with another upon which was written the address of lodgings for Walt. The clerk had done so on purpose. He disliked Wallace Garfield in the same proportions as he liked and admired Walt: all the clerks did. And he did it because he knew he could bury his misconduct deep in the files where it would never be found.

So was this assignment now going to turn to folly on the back of such a devious act? Or had the clerk intuitively seen in Walt, an aging ex-US marshal, something that his superiors had not?

16

MUMBO JUMBO

'What the—'

'Something wrong?' asked the deputy.

The sheriff kept gazing at the *Gazette*. 'Is this a joke?'

The deputy walked over from the counter and looked over the sheriff's shoulder at the full-page advertisement. 'Ten thousand dollars,' he read out loud, slowly, before slurping some coffee from a cream-coloured enamel mug. 'Who's that for?'

The sheriff's eyes darted across the print. 'It's for Justin Roy, the kid from Red Oak who was acquitted last month.'

The deputy went to take another sip of his coffee, but it was near cold, so he decided against it, put the mug down on the desk and leant in closer to read. 'That doesn't make sense,' he said. 'Who would want to put a reward on the head of a man who has been acquitted?'

The sheriff pointed to the name at the bottom. 'A father.'

'Maybe he's just displaying his grief?'

'No,' said the sheriff. 'This goes way beyond grief. This is a reward notice for Justin Roy, dead.'

'You can't do that,' said the deputy as he kept reading. Then he stopped and reread it a second time. 'But it doesn't actually say that. It says it is a proclamation, made in the name of justice against the perpetrator of a grave and fatal injustice against Morris Wilfred Tambling in the County of Bismarck on 4 April 1899.'

'It does between the lines,' said the sheriff.

'But where?'

'There.' The sheriff pointed a little lower down, then read. 'A sum of ten thousand dollars is hereby proclaimed for the delivery of righteousness in the same even proportions.'

'Which means?'

'It is reward for the killing of Justin Roy.'

'But I can't see his name,' said the deputy.

'It doesn't have to be given. The court records are open to the public for all to see and the death of Tambling was widely reported. This is a document that seeks to use legal words to hide its deadly decree, but not its murderous intent.'

'But will anyone understand that?'

'Don't underestimate the lowlife who will be drawn to this madness. They may have to have it read to them and have an explanation of what it means, but word of the bounty will spread like wildfire, and they will know it is an open death warrant.'

'But how will they claim the money?'

'Here, where it says; *And the Lord shall be the true judge of innocence as set out in the scriptures, and may his servants be handsomely rewarded for their services to his righteousness, by being able to proclaim under oath and with the evidence of a photographic image, and any other such personal possessions, that will confirm that justice has been done beyond doubt.*' The sheriff then read the small print at the very bottom of the page. 'All claimants must make their claim to Lawyer Derrick White Harris, attorney for Richard Standley Tambling of Pennsylvania.'

'Sounds like mumbo jumbo,' said the deputy.

But the sheriff wasn't listening. 'I need to send a telegram to the judge so that he may put a stop to this frightful nonsense.'

17

DON'T PAY

'So have you posted my public proclamation?'

'I have, as per your instructions, but against my better judgement. Richard, I wish you would reconsider.'

Tambling's face contorted. 'You were always a timid man. Is it by nature or by profession?'

The lawyer drew breath then exhaled, clearly exasperated by the comment. He went to speak but Tambling was in control. He had made up his mind and was pursuing his purpose with aggression.

'I want you to go out there and ensure momentum does not waver. Keep them awake and on the job.'

'On the job?' said the lawyer.

'Yes, awake and on the job of justice. But I also want to ensure that not one penny is paid until it is confirmed that they have got the right man. Once the body is identified as that of the man who killed my boy, then, and only then will I allow any of the money to be paid out.'

'This is so perilous.' The lawyer's face showed his concern. 'The proclamation has been written in the most careful of legal language, or you would be in contempt of the court that found a defendant not guilty. And what if he is apprehended? Then what? What do we do? The law says he has no case to answer. He must be set free.'

The cold stare of Richard Tambling fixed on the lawyer. 'I've been down there. Down in Kansas and Arkansas, even as far as Texas. My steel is laid upon their prairies and through their towns. I've seen how they work in those parts. They will know the score. They live and die by the gun and believe me, it will be a body we pay on, a dead body. You just need to make sure that they have got the right dead body.'

'Oh Richard, that was a long time ago, those times have passed. These are now communities of law abiding citizens.'

'Have you ever been there, out West?'

'Well, no, but I have read—'

Tambling cut the lawyer short. 'Then you will have read where my boy was gunned down in a saloon. Now does that sound like a community of law abiding citizens?'

'But Richard, what if someone does seek to claim this reward. And what if by mistake they get the wrong man and kill an innocent, what then?'

Tambling fixed his cold stare upon the lawyer. 'That's simple. If they get the wrong man – then they don't get paid.'

18

FIRST CLASS

'Walter, I am going with you.'

Walt looked at the lawyer, his head tilted to one side. 'And why would you want to do that?'

'I have been instructed by Mr Tambling to look after his interests, and he has insisted that I go to Bismarck County.'

Walt squinted. 'You ever been down that way before?'

'No, I have never had that pleasure.'

'Pleasure, ah?' Walt smirked. 'Well, I have, but I've never seen it as a pleasure.' The smirk then turned into a smile. 'Unless I was drunk and sitting in a hot tub with two naked gals. But I don't need to go to Missouri to do that.'

The lawyer sucked in a breath and his face seemed to turn a bright shade of red. 'It could also be for the best, if we are to find and save Mr Roy from those who may seek the reward.'

'We? You plan to go searching with me?'

The lawyer touched his cheek. 'Yes, that is my intention.'

'I don't mind running around the whole of the Louisiana Purchase trying to find your man if that's what is needed, because I'll eventually track him down. It's what I do, and I'm good at it. But if you think. . . .'

The lawyer now lifted his finger from his cheek, to make his point. 'I'm sure you are, Walter, and that's why I have hired your services.'

'Woo-hoo there! Hired my services? I only get paid if I find your man, safe.'

'And you said you will find him, eventually.'

'I'll find him OK. But I've got to do it quick before one of those hundred or so claimants whom your Mr Tambling has let loose, gets to him first. If I don't, then all I'm going to find is a body punctured full of holes.'

The lawyer had a puzzled look on his face. 'A hundred or so? Do you think there will be a hundred men out there seeking the reward?'

'What did you expect?' Walt's tone was matter of fact. 'An old maid and a toothless butler?'

The lawyer now looked confused. 'No, but I really don't know what. . . .' His finger curled and seemed to shrink into his hand. 'But I never thought it would be one hundred. That's an army.'

'It sure is, but they won't be acting like any army. You are going to see every malefactor that ever lived under a rock come out when they get to hear what's on offer. Times are tough and ten thousand dollars is a king's ransom. And if I'm to be successful I need to travel light and fast; not be dragged down by some lawyer.'

'I will pay.'

'Not enough, I'd dare say.'

'A hundred dollars.'

The big ex-marshal scoffed at what he heard.

'A day,' said the lawyer.

Walt seemed to freeze on the spot and looked a little like a statue.

'And I will pay for any expenses, so that will be one hundred dollars in your pocket, for each day.'

Walt slowly came back to life.

'Can you ride?'

'In my day I was an equestrian of note.'

'We'll be riding hard on hired horses, and I don't hire hacks. I'd rather have spirit and pace over manners and a comfortable ride.'

'It will do me good to get back into the saddle again.'

Walt knew this was a stupid idea, but the chance to make one hundred dollars a day was just too inviting. It would be as good as money in the bank, regardless of whether he was able to find Justin Roy or not. If he managed to get just a couple of weeks' work out of it, he would clear close to $1,500. If a month – then $3,000, all for nursemaiding a city lawyer as they rode around the Ozarks looking for a young cowboy. He needed the money and this might be his last chance to get his hands on so much cash, so quickly, and with so little effort. He was too old for ditch digging and he knew it, but that was all he faced as a washed-up ex-marshal with a love for pretty women, Tennessee whiskey and Cuban rum. 'Attorney Harris, I plan on leaving tomorrow on the Union Pacific and have booked a second-class ticket through to St Louis. It leaves at ten, but that's no way for you to travel, so let's say we get there nice and early and rebook our tickets on first class.'

'If you wish, Walter. I'll be there ready for our adventure.'

'Well, dust off those old riding-britches of yours, Counsellor, because once we step off the refinement of the Pullman, it will be bum in the saddle from there on in and until such time as we find your Mr Roy.'

The lawyer was a little taken back by Walter's frank use of language, but he also felt a sense of excitement at the quest that now lay ahead; and such anticipation was something he had not experienced in a long, long time.

19

WILD HOGS

'I don't know if I've ever seen so many reprobates assembled in the one place.'

'You know some of these men?' asked the lawyer.

Walt continued to look around as the faces in the crowd averted their eyes or stepped back to hide behind someone else 'I know some by sight and some by their picture, mostly on a Wanted poster, and I bet if I had a list of names I'd know the rest.'

'Are they all here seeking the reward?'

'This is what the meeting is about. Your Mr Tambling has sent out an open invitation to every deviant and miscreant who makes a living on the wrong side of the law. And these are your acceptances.'

The lawyer looked at the hard unshaven faces of the men. 'Oh dear, what have we done?'

'Geeze, I can tell you that. This is now a ten-thousand dollar turkey shoot and your Mr Roy is the turkey. That's what's been done.'

The lawyer's face went pale.

'Well, now we know,' said Walt.

'Know what?' asked the lawyer in a nervous voice.

'What we are up against.'

'And?'

'The quality is as I expected, mostly trash, but the number is even more than I expected to be here at the start, and numbers, even of trash, can still overwhelm and win on the day.'

The door at the end of the community hall opened to let in the sunlight as the sheriff and the deputy entered.

'Now we'll find out what the law has to say,' said Walt.

The sheriff passed close by Walt and Lawyer Harris as he made his way to the front of the large room, with his deputy just three steps behind, holding his Winchester upright in his right hand. When they got to the small podium the sheriff took off his hat and lifted his hands for silence.

'I'm County Sheriff Ben Ireland and I am going to make an authorized public announcement. The reward posted for the apprehension of Justin Roy, in regard to the killing of Morris Tambling, is illegal in the County of Bismarck. It has been decreed as such by His Honour Judge Ivan Maskell and I expect it will also be illegal in the whole State of Missouri by the end of the week.'

The crowd immediately began to talk, so the sheriff raised his hands again to get quiet.

'The reward is not an authorized state bounty. The man named in the notice was tried in this very room by a county court judge and jury and found not guilty of unlawful killing. If you harm this man in any way, you will be breaking the law.'

'Maybe,' came a yell. 'But sometimes that's what you have to do to get rich.'

The crowd laughed and cheered.

'If you break the law,' said the sheriff, raising his voice, 'you will be held to account by the laws of Missouri and tried in this county.'

'You'd have to arrest us first, Sheriff, and there seems to be more of us than you,' came another yelled response, to be once again cheered by the crowd.

'This is most unseemly,' said the lawyer.

'This is sport,' said Walt. 'It will get unseemly tonight when they all get on the whiskey, and I doubt if the sheriff's cell could hold more than half a dozen men. Even then they would proba-bly need to stand shoulder to shoulder.'

'I guess what you're telling us, Sheriff,' came a shout, 'is that when we get this fella, we will have to take him over the state line to collect our reward.'

The crowd cheered with nodding heads.

'I could see that coming,' said Walt.

'How do we stop them?' asked the lawyer.

'You can't now,' said Walt. 'They've got the smell of money and blood in their nostrils.' Walt looked around. 'And the men-tality of hogs. Wild hogs.'

'So what do we do now?'

'We've got to get to Roy first, and to do that we need to get to the sheriff and try to convince him that we are on his side. That he can trust us.'

'And how do we do that?' asked Harris.

'Hell. You're the lawyer. You're the man who makes his money talking to juries so that they don't hang the guilty. I was hoping you would know what to say.'

'I'm not that sort of lawyer. I don't practise criminal law. I deal with business and commerce law.'

Walt gave a huffing sound, dug his thumbs in behind his gunbelt, then lifted it a little. 'Well don't ask me. I shoot better than I talk. When I was a marshal, my job was to get them into the court, not to make depositions.'

20

UPSET

'Sheriff,' Walt called, but the sheriff kept walking. He called again. 'Sheriff.'

Sheriff Ireland kept walking, but glanced back over his shoulder, then stopped. 'What is it?'

Walt slowed into a walk and was a little out of breath. 'We want to give you a hand.'

'What makes you think I need one?' The sheriff was now looking Walt and the lawyer up and down.

'We were at the meeting. We got to see your problem first hand.'

'If you were at the meeting then it seems to me that you are part of that problem.'

Walt sucked in a breath and came to a halt in front of the sheriff. He offered his hand. 'Walt Garfield, ex-US marshal, now working for this gentleman here, Lawyer Derrick Harris of Pittsburgh.'

The sheriff had just grasped Walt's hand in a strong grip only to let it drop, as if he had picked up the hot end of branding-iron. 'Harris? Lawyer Harris of Pittsburgh?'

The lawyer was standing back a little and to one side of Walt. He nodded and smiled.

'I know Harris by name.' The sheriff looked across at the lawyer with a cold stare. 'I wrote to you to notify the next of kin of Morris Tambling's death, and I saw your name on the proclamation.'

'Yes, I thank you for your correspondence,' said the lawyer.

Walt tried to smile. 'So you two kind of know each other already?'

'What I know,' said the sheriff, 'is that Harris is mixed up in this idiocy.'

'Well, yes I am,' said the lawyer. 'But I am here with Marshal Garfield to make things right.'

'Ex-marshal,' corrected Walt, but the sheriff wasn't listening. All his attention was on the lawyer.

'Put things right?' The sheriff's voice was raised. 'If you want to put things right, then revoke the reward, immediately.'

'If only I could, Sheriff. But the instructions and the funding of the reward are the business of Richard Tambling, the father of Morris. He's upset.'

'Upset?' the word came from the sheriff's mouth like a freight train letting off steam. He stepped in towards the lawyer and was now less than one pace away from Walt. 'Upset? I'll give you upset.'

Walt pulled his head back a little and was thankful the sheriff was taking aim at the lawyer and not him.

'I have over two hundred armed, degenerate, troublemakers in this town with only one thing on their mind, killing an innocent man so that they may claim enough money to stay drunk and go whoring till they fall over dead. I've just told them that the reward is invalid here in Bismarck County, but they couldn't care less. If they find Roy they will still kill him, then drag the body over the county or state line. It will make no difference to them. They'll even drag the body all the way to Pittsburgh and into your Mr Richard Tambling's parlour if they have to. And tonight me and my deputy will have to keep this town safe from this rabble that you have assembled. So if you want to see upset . . .' the sheriff stepped in closer to the lawyer and was now almost nose to nose, 'then look at me.'

The lawyer's mouth opened, but nothing came out.

The sheriff turned and walked away at a brisk pace.

'Well, that went well,' said Walt facetiously.

The lawyer seemed frozen to the spot, his eyes wide and mouth slightly open. 'I've, I've—' His mouth closed then opened again. 'I've . . . never been spoken to like that before in my life. He must be very upset.'

'Yeah,' said Walt. 'I kinda got the same impression.'

21

TITTLE-TATTLE

Walt stopped and stood in the doorway for a moment before he leant in to knock against the inside wall. 'Sheriff,' he called, announcing himself.

The sheriff looked up. 'What do you want?'

Walt lifted his hands up to shoulder height with the palms forward. 'Whoa there; I'm on your side, really. I'm here to help, if you just give me thirty seconds to have my say.' He took a step into the sheriff's office. 'Then if you want to throw me out the door or throw me in a cell, you can go right ahead.'

The sheriff dropped his head slightly and pursed his lips in annoyance.

Walt took the silence as a good sign. 'I think I can help you with keeping your town safe.'

The sheriff's eyes narrowed to show that he was sceptical of any such proposition.

'I know most of the reprobates who have come to your town by name. I also know that most of them are still wanted on outstanding warrants for felony charges in Kansas, Kentucky, Tennessee, Arkansas and Iowa.'

The sheriff said nothing, but Walt had his attention.

'I suggest that you put the word out that you are going to start serving those writs.'

The sheriff lifted his head. 'I don't have the time to go getting interstate warrants, and I don't have the cell space to lock up more than eight men.'

'I figured that, but I didn't say that you actually had to serve any warrants, I just said that you put the word out that you are going to.'

'What good will that do?'

Walt advanced two steps as he spoke. 'If any of these boys get a whiff that they are about to be served upon, then they will do what they always do: move on, fast, to keep at least one pace ahead of the law.'

'That still doesn't provide any safety for the young man with the reward on his head.'

'No, it doesn't, but first things first. Let's make the town safe, then we can address saving Roy's hide.'

'How do you propose to get the word out that I'm about to start serving warrants?'

Walt thought for a moment and used the time to advance another two steps. 'What's your most popular saloon?'

'The Silver Eagle,' said the deputy.

'You got a reliable man behind the bar who could pass on a little gossip? A little tittle-tattle he heard from a reliable source, that a US Marshal has arrived with a lawyer to assist the sheriff in identifying felons on outstanding warrants.'

Again it was the deputy who responded. 'Stan Lynch,' he said.

Walt looked at the sheriff, trying to get a sign as to whether he agreed.

The sheriff remained mute.

'This Lynch, you think he could do it?' asked Walt.

The sheriff still didn't move or say a word.

'If I gave you the names,' added Walt.

Still the sheriff didn't move.

Walt shrugged and half-turned to go.

'Stan owes me,' said the sheriff. 'He'll do it.'

'Good.' Walt smiled with relief. 'You might like to start with the Sutton boys, three brothers and a cousin. Wanted for cattle-duffing in Arkansas. The warrant was drawn up in Fort Smith. Also outstanding are warrants from Fort Worth for Des Spencer and Billy Riley; they are wanted for questioning over a mail car robbery on the Katy, over near Waco, that goes back nearly five years. From Tennessee you have Pat Harrison, Jude Radford and Lenny Griffiths. I also saw the Frenchman Blereau in the crowd, which was a surprise because I'd heard he'd run foul of a gambling syndicate over in Chattanooga and been thrown off a riverboat. Looks like he's a swimmer. He relieved some folks in Bowling Green of their life savings. You want me to keep going?'

The sheriff looked over at the deputy. 'Get a pad and pencil, Jim, so we can start taking down some of these names.'

Walt smiled again and stepped up to the counter.

22

MOVING TARGETS

Walt was back at the sheriff's office the following morning, leaning over the counter and examining a list of names with the deputy.

'So you can tick off the Sutton boys. They left before the saloon closed. Radford and the Frenchman were in the boarding house where I'm staying and they left last night as well, which means I can move from the tent out the back and into an upstairs room.'

'Dan over at the Lake Street livery said that most of his stalls were empty this morning, but he's not concerned, as he had everyone pay in advance,' reported the deputy.

'Now that's a wise man,' said Walt. 'Just hope he checked the colour of their money.'

The deputy had a questioning look on his face.

'In case the ink runs if the notes get wet.'

The deputy understood. 'Have some dealt in counterfeit?'

'The Frenchman has. And so has Riley. But that was a while back. I think they all prefer to deal the real thing nowadays.'

'I've never seen a forged banknote,' said the deputy.

'You may have,' said Walt. 'Some are so good it takes a man with a technical eye and a magnifying glass to tell the difference. Although it's often the paper that is the big giveaway; when you rub it between your fingers it just doesn't seem right. But hell, who does that when you're in a saloon or pressing yourself against a good-looking gal?'

The deputy's face went a little pink just as the sheriff stepped into the office.

Walt smiled but got nothing back in return. 'Worked a treat,' he said. 'We are just crossing off the names. I had no trouble getting a beer last night after your man put out the word. And those who have stayed seem to be on best behaviour.'

The sheriff put his hat on the wall peg, but didn't say anything.

'We need to talk about Roy,' said Walt.

'Well, hopefully that's been taken care of as well.'

'How come?' asked Walt.

'If those who are concerned about being served a warrant left town, then hopefully they will have left the county, even the state.'

Walt shook his head. 'I doubt it. I'd say they have just gone to ground. While that reward is still posted, they will be buzzing around looking for the honeypot.'

'Then get that lawyer of yours to remove the pot.'

'He would if he could, but he can't. That's why Lawyer Harris hired me. Tambling is a man with money and the urge to kill and this is how wealthy men do it. They get someone else to perform the dirty work for them. It's sort of neat and easy that way. They all like the smell and taste of blood, but they just don't have the stomach to make it run.'

'How come you know so much?'

The sheriff's voice told Walt that he was not in a good mood, so he tried to use all the charm he could muster and smiled. 'I was marshal for twenty-seven years. Left just over a year ago. I've worked around this neck of the woods, not in your county, but I know the country. Know the riffraff that inhabitants it even better. Most have gone through the courts, somewhere, but each year they get smarter and harder.'

'Is that why you left?'

It was an insult, but Walt didn't let it get to him. 'The old ones I can still handle. It's the young ones who are the trouble. They get faster while I'm getting slower. A lot of them also have a mean streak, and the only way to deal with mean is to match it. Me, well I'm too genteel for all that now.' Walt grinned. 'Well, at least most of the time.'

The sheriff nodded and Walt took it as a good sign. 'Harris hired me to find Roy and take him to safety. Says he'll pay me handsomely if I can, and I tell you, the marshal service didn't pay me enough to sit on a front porch in my old age.'

'So how do you plan to keep him safe if you find him?'

'Ah,' said Walt. 'That's the rub, isn't it? You and I know he will never be safe until the bounty is withdrawn, and while I have some ideas about that, it's not my immediate concern.'

'What is?' asked the sheriff, lifting his head a little as he spoke.

'I've got to find him first and that may take time. I don't think we have much of that. If someone else finds him first, then he's a dead man.' Walt was looking squarely at the sheriff.

'So?'

'So, are you going to tell me where he is?'

'And why would I do that?'

'Because you don't want an innocent man killed. I can see it. It's in your character and it came out when you gave the lawyer that spray. You're concerned about the boy.'

'I'll look after it myself,' said the sheriff.

'Ahhh,' said Walt. 'So you are planning on riding to his rescue?'

The sheriff said nothing.

'Well at least let me and the lawyer travel with you.' Walt watched the sheriff carefully and saw a mannerism that he had noticed during the meeting at the community hall, just before Ireland spoke to the crowd. He had also seen it again when they had first met, and he saw it now. The sheriff pressed his lips tightly together, then sucked back slightly. It was a tiny sign that he was thinking, deciding what to say or do, and Walt saw it as his chance – the opportunity to persuade.

'That way,' said Walt, 'you get the best of both worlds. Someone to share the load as well as extra reinforcements in case some of those marauding proclaimers decide to bushwhack you.'

The sheriff sucked back a little and the air made a whistling sound over his lips.

'Besides,' said Walt. 'What are you going to do with him? You can't bring him back here. You have to protect him until we can get that reward revoked.'

The sheriff set his eyes on Walt. 'When I leave here, I'll be travelling hard.'

'I expected that.'

'And I won't tell you where I am going until we get there.'

'A man who understands security; I like that.'

'And I can't see any need to bring the lawyer.'

'Well, I used to think that myself,' said Walt. 'But I've had a change of mind, on reflection, and now I know what we are up against. He's the only one with a direct link to the man who can pay or rescind the reward. Without him, we'll be no more than a moving target that's getting in the way of ten thousand dollars in prize money to the first person who can knock us off, so that they can get to young Roy. Now, I'm not much one for lawyers myself, but this one could be powerful handy. So taking him along would seem to make a lot of sense, to me.' Walt grinned. 'What about you?'

23

ADVENTURE

'I'm going to have to hire me some horses and get some provisions, so do you want to let me in on how far we are planning to go, Sheriff?'

'You'll need two horses each. I plan to ride by day, rest up by night. The towns we'll be going through are well provisioned, but bring a bedroll, coffee and hardtack; the rest we can get on the way. I'm carrying the coffee pot and a skillet, but that's all.'

'Travelling light,' said Walt, to confirm that he had got the message.

'And fast. I want to do no less than forty miles a day, by the crow.'

'And how many days would that be?' asked Walt.

The sheriff looked at Walt like a schoolmaster who had just been asked by one of his students what questions he was proposing to include in a forthcoming test.

'I didn't ask where,' said Walt. 'I didn't even ask in what direction, I just asked for how long. So I can plan, and let the lawyer know how many saddle sores he's going to get.'

'Four.'

'Four,' repeated Walt. 'Good.'

'And water,' said the sheriff. 'At least two canteens each, just in case.'

'Just in case,' Walt repeated back. 'Two cans each.' But his mind was preoccupied with the ground that lay in a radius of 160 miles upon the map to the north, south, east and west. If it were to the east it would be the country around Springfield. To the west was Topeka, Silver Lake area. To the south it was Joplin, and to the north, Knoxville. All places he knew.

When he saw the lawyer he addressed him as if he was a young deputy newly assigned.

Lawyer Harris responded in return with enthusiasm. 'And what personal items should I purchase for the journey?' he asked.

Walt looked him up and down. 'You can go like you are, but that suit is going to be ruined. I would suggest comfort. I like my trousers real baggy around the knees, seat and crotch.'

The lawyer seemed to be taken somewhat aback.

'So, I'd keep your jacket and shirt, but get some new breeches.' Walt looked down to the lawyer's feet. 'Your boots look OK, but they won't be as shiny in a day or two.'

'I'd like a new hat,' said the lawyer. 'One like yours.'

'You'll pay through the nose for a new hat out here, but the general store will have 'em.'

'I would like your assistance, Walter, when I purchase.'

'Why not? I'll select and you pay.'

'And then we will set off on our adventure.'

'Yes, an adventure, I suppose,' said Walt, not quite sure what else to say.

'Like the knights of the round table.'

'Ah, yeah,' said Walt slowly, 'just like them. I guess.' But as he pushed his hat back and scratched his forehead, he couldn't help but wonder what the hell Sir Lancelot had to do with the next four days in the saddle. Four days of twelve to fourteen-hours each depending on the country, bouncing your balls up and down on the leather so that a young cowboy, who had been let off by the law, wasn't going to be hunted down and lynched by the lawless.

Was it an adventure? Well, yes, he thought, I suppose it is. Maybe he'd just forgotten what an adventure was, and maybe he also needed to go back and take another look at King Arthur and his gallant knights, just in case he and Lancelot had a lot in common.

24

CHIVALRY

The three riders and six horses left just before dawn. The sheriff led the way, as only he knew the direction in which they would be travelling. Walt waved to the lawyer to follow close behind the sheriff, so that he himself could then tag along as the last man, and be in a position from which to observe and think. But Lawyer Harris kept falling back, so Walt rode up to his side to gee him up, only to find a most uncomfortable man.

'Problems?' asked Walt.

'Can't seemed to find my stride,' said the lawyer.

'Leave that up to the horse,' said Walt. He leant over and grabbed the cheek-strap of the halter on the lawyer's horse. 'Important we keep up and don't slow the sheriff down; we have a long way to go and he's planning on forty miles by this evening.' Walt pulled the horse from a slow walk up to a trot and the lawyer seemed to bounce out of rhythm with every stride, his seat slapping up and down upon the saddle.

'I don't know if I am up to this,' said Harris with a pained look on his face.

'No choice,' said Walt. 'The deal is a simple one. He leads and we follow. And he has no intention of slowing down.'

The lawyer grimaced. 'Forty miles a day? Oh God!'

'God won't help,' said Walt. 'He travels in a coach drawn by angels.' He winked at the lawyer, who forced an agonized smile in return. 'That's the way,' said Walt with cheer. 'It's just a matter of grinning and bearing it, ah?'

The lawyer tried to grin and speak, but it just came out as a weak simper.

They stopped for water mid-morning and the sheriff calculated that they had covered about eight miles. Walt thought that was about right, which put them two miles behind their planned timetable. By noon they had covered another eight and half, so were now three and half miles behind the sheriff's intention to be halfway by midday. He expressed his dissatisfaction with the state of affairs, but Walt laughed it off, saying that it was a known fact that lawyers always rode fastest towards the setting sun.

'But we're travelling north,' said the sheriff.

'I noticed,' said Walt as he thought of the towns that lay ahead.

In the early afternoon they passed through a cattle camp, where the sheriff quickly dismounted to pay his respects. Walt wasn't privy to the conversation, but as he watched from the saddle it seemed that the sheriff was enquiring as to any traffic that might have passed. If his assumption was right, then the sheriff was concerned that some of the reward hunters might already be on the trail and heading in the right direction.

Walt hoped that the sheriff would confide in him by offering up what he had been told, but nothing came forth, so he said,

'Any word?'

The response was a simple, 'Nope.'

Walt thought for a moment, but for the life of him he couldn't think of anything to say that would prompt a conversation.

By mid afternoon the lawyer had seemed to fall into a trance. His face was covered with white dust, giving him a ghostly look that reminded Walt of a circus act he had seen years before when chasing a family of mule-rustlers south of Omaha. He had stopped on seeing the big tent, only out of casual interest, and was offered a free ticket to make up the poor numbers. The show was half-over as he slid on to the wood bench in time to see an old clown jump, bareback, upon a white pony. The comic was dressed as a Chinaman and rode the horse in a tight circle around the small ring, while the ring-master cracked a long whip at his false pigtail as it floated in the air behind him. The rider showed no emotion whatsoever upon his face as the thin leather popper flicked dangerously close to his head. The crowd roared with laughter, but not Walt. He knew pluck when he saw it. This was a dangerous act for a few thoughtless laughs and a pauper's miserable wage, and it convinced Walt that life as a US marshal wasn't half as bad as he thought.

True to his word, the sheriff made sure that they covered their forty miles, but it was nearly two hours after sunset by the time they arrived in Gallatin. Walt pulled himself from the saddle, stretched, rubbed the small of his back and walked across to the lawyer. He patted an open hand against the leather boot that was still in the stirrup and said, 'One down, three to go.'

Lawyer Harris let out a moan in response.

'Don't be like that,' said Walt. 'It can only get easier from here.'

But it didn't.

The lawyer certainly seemed to sleep well that first night in a canvas cot at the Jade Guesthouse, but when he went to rise he found that he had seized up in every part of his body. 'I can't seem to get anything to bend.'

'I've been like that,' said Walt. 'A good night in the sack with a young gal can do that to an old man.' He laughed loudly, but got no immediate response.

After a bit the lawyer said, 'That sort of riding is far more enjoyable than what we are doing.'

The comment surprised Walt, but tickled his fancy no end.

The second day passed in much the same way as the first, with them making Bethany just after last light. Lawyer Harris did his best to make light conversation, albeit through gritted teeth. However, on the third day the lawyer was completely silent. Then, when they rose for the fourth day, at Bedford, he seemed to come good, quietly checking each of his horses with silent, but meticulous care in the half-light.

'Just forty to go,' said Walt. 'To. . . ?' He was trying to think of what town lay forty miles to the north-east, as that had been their track.

'Red Oak,' said the lawyer.

'Yes,' said Walt. 'It would be around Red Oak.'

'No, it is Red Oak.' The lawyer's voice was unaccustomedly firm.

Walt was a little taken back by the certainty of the destination.

'Red Oak,' repeated Walt. 'You sure?'

'It is where Justin Roy comes from, it was in the court transcripts.'

Walt thought for a moment. 'Right,' he said slowly. 'Now is there anything else you would like to share with me, because I have been racking my brains trying to figure where we were going.'

'Only that I think the sheriff is a good man. He sincerely wishes to protect this young cowboy.'

'Right,' said Walt. 'That's most useful to know. So we should all get along famously.' The remark was made lightly.

However, the lawyer's response was serious. 'Yes, we should,' he said. 'I think we can now all act with chivalry.'

'Right,' said Walt slowly, now a little lost. 'Like those gallant knights?'

But the lawyer didn't seem to understand what Walt was talking about.

25

MISTAKEN IDENTITY

The sheriff of Red Oak was out of town, leaving his deputy, a hesitant young man, in charge. Walt and Lawyer Harris had accompanied Sheriff Ireland to the office, but now kept their respectful distance as the two conversed. For Walt this was a painful situation as he wanted to know what was being said, but no matter how hard he strained to hear, he was only able to pick up the odd word. This hearing affliction had been with him since the war, when as a nineteen-year-old he had been stationed with his platoon as flank protection to the brigade's artillery. For three days the guns had pounded the Federal advance upon Chancellorsville and when they eventually stopped with Hooker's retreat back across the Rappahannock River, he found that he and all his fellow soldiers had a slight but permanent ringing in their ears. It didn't much worry him at first. After all, it was a common complaint, but as the years went on it seemed to get a little worse, and at times like these, it was impossible to listen in to the conservation that was taking place on the other side of the sheriff's office.

'I wish I could hear what they are talking about,' he said to the lawyer.

'I think the sheriff is confiding in the young man. Telling him we are here to find Justin Roy.'

'I guessed that,' said Walt, 'but it's what the deputy is saying that I'm interested in.'

'He looks a little ill at ease,' said Lawyer Harris.

'He's skittish, all right,' said Walt as he watched the adolescent lawman.

'Maybe it's because his sheriff is away?'

'No, I don't think so.' Walt was speaking from experience. 'Normally a deputy loves to have his sheriff away, gives him a chance to rule the roost, to be number one. Unless. . . .'

'Unless what?'

'Unless he's expecting trouble that he doesn't believe he can handle.'

Only later that evening was the truth revealed, when the sheriff of Red Oak returned and came to the Lucky Horseshoe boarding house to awake the three men.

'My deputy has told me that you have travelled from Bismarck County to protect Justin Roy.'

Sheriff Ireland identified himself and then introduced Harris and Walt to the Red Oak sheriff, before confirming that that was their intention.

'Well, you're too late.'

Sheriff Ireland's eyes showed his concern before he spoke. 'Is he dead?' he asked.

'No, but he is on the run and I think it will only be a matter of time before he is dead.'

'Why do you say that?' asked Walt.

The sheriff turned his gaze on Walt. 'His neighbours, the Allens, have a boy about the same age. He was shot down in cold blood yesterday evening.'

Walt nodded that he understood. 'Did you get who did it?'

'No, they left straight after the shooting without rendering any help, even though they realized that they had shot the wrong man, once they had questioned him. Didn't even plug the wound to give him a chance. No word to anyone: they just rode away. By the time he was found, he was all but gone. All he was able to do was tell what happened and pass on his farewell to his mother.'

The lawyer was confused and went to speak, but Walt put out a hand and rested it upon Harris's arm to quieten him.

'Do you know where Justin Roy has gone?' asked Sheriff Ireland.

'No I don't,' said the Red Oak sheriff. 'But if he has any sense it will be far away from here, because I suspect there will be more people looking for him.'

'I'd suspect that too,' agreed Walt, who hoped that Sheriff Ben Ireland wasn't about to inform the sheriff of Red Oak about the 200 townsfolk whom he had addressed in the Bismarck County community hall.

The sheriff of Red Oak scuffed the floor with a sharp kick of his boot. 'If I could find the son-of-bitch who set this bounty on an innocent man, I'd string him up myself.'

The lawyer shuffled his feet in his turn and was about to speak; once again Walt quietened him with a hand upon his sleeve.

When the two sheriffs left the boarding house to stand on the street and converse, Harris said to Walt. 'I needed to ask.'

'What exactly?'

The lawyer thought for a moment. 'I'm a little confused.'

'Why is that?' said Walt, as he looked through the window at the silhouettes of two lawmen deep in conversation.

'What has the death of the neighbour's boy got to do with Justin Roy?'

'Mistaken identity.' Walt turned and looked around the room. 'Do you feel like a whiskey?' He bent at the knees and seemed to swivel on the spot, searching for the alcoholic beverage, should it magically appear in their room.

'No,' said the lawyer. 'I try to keep my consumption to times of necessity.' He watched Walt as he kept searching. 'Mistaken identity, how?'

'Some of those lowlife proclaimers chasing that big fat reward shot down the wrong man. They went to the wrong farm, saw someone who they thought was Justin Roy and shot him down. Seems he was still alive and was able to tell them who he really was so they ran off, leaving him for dead.'

'Oh,' said the lawyer. 'That's what I thought, but just couldn't believe such a thing could happen.'

'It has, and it does, and it will again. Trigger-happy lowlife, who shoot first then ask if they got the right man.' Walt sat down on the side of the steel framed bed and began to put on his boots. 'I'm going to find a drink,' he declared.

The lawyer hung his head and his shoulders sagged, as if he'd been crushed. 'Walter, this is a terrible affair. A young innocent man has been killed and his family must now mourn his passing for their lifetime.'

'Yep,' said the old ex-marshal as he tugged his boot on to his foot.

'Walter?' It was said as if to ask a question.

Walter stood up and stamped his foot to make the boot fit. 'What?'

'I'll come with you. I need a drink too.'

26

NOTHING BUT TEARS

She had that used-up look, which came from years of hard work and little hope. The sun, wind and cold had each taken their toll upon her face and now it was heavily lined, but her eyes remained wide and clear to show both her pride and her hurt.

She stood on the porch, watching, absolutely still, with her right hand held just below the hairline to shade her eyes from the glare, as the four horsemen rode towards her. The two sheriffs dismounted and walked quickly to her, as Walt swung out of the saddle slowly and removed his hat as a sign of respect.

Sheriff Ireland was introduced to the woman by the sheriff from Red Oak, but Walt and Lawyer Harris were left to stand, like shags on a rock, watching and out of earshot. The meeting had come about at Walt's insistence, in the hope that Justin Roy's mother would tell them where he might have fled. When the two sheriffs turned away from the woman it was evident to Walt that they were no wiser as to his whereabouts. As soon as they mounted, he moved forward and introduced himself with a soft handshake.

'Ma'am, me and that lawyer over there can save your boy.'

'So Sheriff Darcy Townsend said.' Her voice showed no emotion.

'But we have to find him first.'

'I told the sheriff I don't know where he has gone. My boy said it would be best that way. If I didn't know, then I couldn't tell anyone, by mistake.'

'That's smart,' said Walt.

'He can be, when he's not being foolish.'

'That goes for all of us, ma'am, no matter how young or old we are.' Walt saw the pride on her face amongst the lines of concern. He looked around the small farmyard. 'You here on your own?'

'Just me now.'

'You need him back here then.'

Her head nodded, just slightly.

Walt looked directly into her eyes. 'Help me to find your boy.'

She looked away, over Walt's shoulder, towards the three mounted riders. Walt threw a quick glance over his shoulder and they all looked impatient, with their horses half turned ready to leave.

'When he was a boy, where did he go to hunt?'

Justin Roy's mother stood mute, her hand still shading her eyes.

Walt nodded in recognition to her silence. 'Thank you,' he said. 'I won't bother you any more.' He turned, pulling the brim of his hat down as he stepped off towards his horse.

'Mister.'

Walt wasn't sure if he heard her call but he stopped and turned.

'Ma'am?' he said.

'Can you return my boy safe and sound?'

Walt pushed his hat back a little. 'If I find him, I can.'

'Try Honey Creek; his father use to take the boys up there – it was their prize for working hard. Our Justin loved it best of all. It has good memories for him. He'll feel safe up there.'

'Honey Creek,' said Walt, and once again pulled on the brim of his hat in acknowledgement. 'Thank you for your trust. If I can find him quick, I will keep him safe. It may mean that I have to hide him away for a little while before I get him back to you, but that's just how it has to be.'

'A little while I can stand, for ever I can't. He's the last of my boys and his father passed on while he was still a lad. I have no one else.'

'I understand.'

When Walt had pulled himself back into the saddle the lawyer asked what had been said.

'The stakes have just been raised,' Walt answered, without looking at the lawyer.

'How so?'

Walt now caught the lawyer's eye. 'All she has is her boy. If he is killed she will be left with nothing but tears, an empty heart and a farm that will eventually kill her.'

The lawyer looked back over his shoulder at the solitary figure standing on the porch. 'The hand of Providence can be pitiless,' he said.

'Well, it certainly doesn't help when that hand is throwing around ten thousand dollars to every degenerate this side of the Mississippi, to kill her boy.'

The lawyer opened his mouth to speak, then screwed up his face and said nothing, but Walt knew his small scolding had not been lost on the man. The lawyer was learning what life was like away from the big city and his privileged life. Out here justice was random and harsh.

27

BLIND FAITH

'Honey Creek? Yeah, I know Honey Creek. But she didn't say anything to me about Honey Creek.' The sheriff of Red Oak was showing his irritation as he watered his horse from the roadside trough at the turn-off back to town.

Walt didn't care. 'Maybe you didn't ask?'

Walt's response clearly annoyed the sheriff even more and it showed when he spoke. 'I asked her if she knew where her boy was, and she said, no. So I say we go east.'

'East?' Walt said it in a tone as if he had just heard an idiot comment.

Lawyer Harris edged into Walt's view to catch his eye. Walt saw the look on the lawyer's face, which showed his concern at the two men going head to head. Walt also saw that Sheriff Ireland was about to intervene, so he relented just a little and softened his tone. 'She said she didn't know to me, too, but that was because her boy wouldn't tell her. Hell, she didn't want to know either, just in case she pointed the finger at where he might be, unintentionally.'

The sheriff now backed off just a little. 'So how did you find out, then?'

'I asked where her boy liked to go hunting.'

The lawyer caught Walt's eye, again.

Walt saw the look on the attorney's face and got the message. Lawyer Harris wanted him to be more appeasing, so he turned his head away and rubbed the side of his face, letting his fingers fan across his chin and his thumb scratch against the stubble on his cheek. He knew it was frustration. He liked to work on his own and get things done his way and without delay, but here, with a lawyer and two county sheriffs, he felt fenced in. He told himself to cool down and took in a long breath.

'I figured that he would go and hide in a place that he knew, and one not too far from his mother and the farm.'

The sheriff looked down, scuffed a foot in the dirt, raising a little powdered dust, but remained silent.

Walt dropped his hand and tucked a thumb into his belt. 'He's just returned home with his tail between his legs and I don't think he wants to go anywhere. But he has no choice; he knows he's being chased.'

The sheriff scuffed the other foot. 'Makes sense,' he conceded in a mumble.

The lawyer had moved into a position behind the sheriff's left shoulder, so that Walt couldn't help but see the silent signals he was sending from his penetrating eyes.

What? he mouthed while the sheriff was looking down.

The lawyer was now nodding with wide eyes.

Walt finally got the message; it was one of offering more appeasement. 'It was just a long shot,' he said lowering his voice. 'But I thought it was worth a try or we'll go chasing our tails.'

The sheriff gave a slight nod in agreement.

Walt paused and glanced over at the lawyer, who was now bobbing his head with approval. 'But I don't know the country,

I've never heard of Honey Creek, so . . .' he paused, 'so I could do with some . . .' He paused again, but didn't look at the lawyer because this three-way conversation was starting to annoy him. 'Some help to find this boy,' he said at last.

The sheriff nodded. 'I know Honey Creek. It's pretty this time of the year, but harsh in winter. Fishing and hunting are good, and there are places to hide, I'll give you that. Lots of gullies too, but rocky though.'

'Far?' asked Walt.

'A day's ride, not much more.'

'Direction?'

'North, then a little east, towards Nebraska.'

'Any farms up that way?'

'A few, but mostly to the south and west of the creek. It's not friendly farming country and the east and north are the most rugged. Some miners get up there from time to time, but I don't think they have ever found anything much. There is the odd squatter's shack, but only the resourceful stay all year round. This time of year it is OK. Even see Nebraskans fishing and shooting there.'

'And soon some proclaimers,' said Walt.

The sheriff seemed a little surprised. 'Why would anyone think of going to Honey Creek to find Justin Roy?' As he spoke, his hand brushed the top of his ear to chase off a sandfly.

'Believe me, Sheriff,' said Walt, 'where there's money, lots of money, you'll find someone who is able to figure out where to go to find it. Even the most dim-witted of these idiots seem to have a knack for it. I guess they must smell it, or something. I've come to the realization that what the simple-minded lack in smarts, they make up by being cunning and devious. And they are annoying, like that gnat.'

The sheriff brushed his ear again. 'Sheriff Ireland said you were once in the law yourself.'

'Once.'

'Miss it?'

'Sometimes, but only when I forget.'

'Forget what?'

'Forget what it's like to be wet, cold, tired, hungry and saddle-sore, while chasing after some miscreant who was released by a penitentiary parole board that doesn't know sense from shit. Then, and only then, do I miss it.'

The sheriff smiled. 'Yeah, it can be like that, can't it?'

'Can it ever!'

'So this is a bit different for you, then?'

Walt was a little puzzled by the question. 'Different? Hell, I'm used to this. It's just that I'm getting too old for it. That's all.'

'No, I don't mean that. I mean, trying to stop a killing before it happens. Prevention, like.'

'Prevention?' said Walt, pausing to consider the word. 'Yeah, I guess it is.'

'Do you think you can?'

Walt squinted in response to the query. He was confused again.

'Do you think you can prevent this boy from being killed?'

Walt thought for a moment. 'If I find him I can keep him safe – for a while, but truth is I can't stop him from being killed in six months or a year's time. Nobody can, not until that prize is taken away. He has a death sentence hanging over his head. In fact, he might as well be riding around with a noose around his neck, just waiting for one of those proclaimers to jerk it tight.'

'So what are you going to do?'

Walt shrugged. 'I've got myself a lawyer.' Walt looked over at Lawyer Harris who smiled, so Walt smiled back.

The sheriff saw where Walt was looking and turned his head to acknowledge the lawyer, whom he hadn't seen standing behind and just off to one side. Then he turned back to Walt slowly and leant in close. 'Can a lawyer fix this?' he said in a whisper.

'Have you ever seen a lawyer fix anything?' whispered Walt in return.

The sheriff thought for a moment or two then said. 'Can't say I have. What about you?'

Walt slowly shook his head in response. 'Nope, me neither.'

'So where's your faith come from?' asked the Sheriff of Red Oak.

Walt pondered a little. 'I guess it's just blind faith at the moment, but that's all I've got, so I have to run with it.'

28

TRACKS

Walt had it in his mind that he would look out for any sign that Justin Roy might have left when travelling from Red Oak to Honey Creek. If he could pick up his tracks maybe they would lead straight to his hideout. But he quickly realized that this was one of his more foolish notions, as the road they were travelling on was good, hard, and well worn. Thankfully, he hadn't mentioned his intentions to the two sheriffs, whom he happened to overhear as they talked about this very subject.

'You ever done much tracking?' asked Sheriff Ireland.

'You mean when trying to follow up someone?'

Ireland confirmed that's what he meant.

'I have,' said the sheriff from Red Oak. 'But unless it's a four-wheeled wagon pulled by three or four oxen across a sandy plain, then I can't say I've been able to follow up anybody, especially if they are covering their tracks.'

'No Indian, ah?' said Ireland.

'I've heard the stories about people who can follow a man on foot a month after he has passed, but I've never seen it,' confided Sheriff Townsend.

The truth was, nor had Walt, except for one brief occasion. He had worked with some Indian scouts over the years who were very good, but even they were the first to dampen any expectations of success, especially where the trail was more than a day or two old. The exception had been when he was part of a posse that had tracked down a lost girl; and her life had been saved solely by the abilities of an Indian tracker.

It had happened not long after he had joined the marshal service in 1870, when he decided to assist a local sheriff as a way of showing appreciation for his previous support in apprehending a horse thief. He knew that he was just making up numbers in the search party, but so were most of the others. The Indian tracker was a Mandan Sioux, one of the few to survive the smallpox epidemic that had reduced their tribe to less than 150. He was an older man who kept to himself, but he was also happy to speak when engaged, one on one. Trouble was nobody seemed to want to speak to him, even though he was put out front to find the child's trail.

The local sheriff who was in charge of the posse thought that the Indian was taking too long, as he had dismounted to lead his horse on foot, stopping from time to time to squat and examine the ground. So the sheriff made a snap decision and rode on with the posse in tow. Walt had dismounted and was adjusting his saddle when they departed in a haze of dust and beating hoofs through the low brush. The Indian was kneeling just off to one side, looking at a small tuft of prairie grass when they left without warning. He slowly stood to watch their departure. Although not intentionally, the sheriff's actions had humiliated the old man, who up to that point had been leading the direction of the search. Walt thought it necessary to stay, but wasn't sure what to say at that very moment.

The Indian waited until the departing crowd had disappeared, although they could still be heard thumping through the undergrowth, before he turned to Walt with a smile and said. 'Now there are tracks that I can follow.'

Walt couldn't stop himself from smiling at the old warrior's humour. He had always seen wit, when used under difficulty and aimed at oneself, as a sign of an unbreakable spirit. He had first experienced it during the war as a young soldier when wiser and older heads could still force a grin during the gravest of circumstances, and he had found it an attractive and uplifting quality.

'I guess they're a little impatient,' he said in the sheriff's defence.

'Well, they're going to get even more impatient, because the child has not gone in that direction,' said the tracker softly.

'You can see the sign?' asked Walt.

'No, I've lost it at the moment,' said the old man. 'But the child is wandering in a wide circle to the right, not a straight line, so they won't find her where they are going. I just need to keeping looking as I follow that circle and I will pick up some sign, sometime.'

Walt mounted, but sat and waited.

The Indian said. 'You should go with the sheriff.'

Walt glanced at the dust in the distance, then said. 'No, I think I'll stay with you.'

The Indian showed no emotion at the declaration. He just said. 'Then best we walk together so that our eyes are close to the ground.'

Walt dismounted and followed along and sure enough, about a quarter of a mile later, the Indian started to pick up some sign where the child had started to follow a narrow sandy animal trail. He pointed to scuff marks, small stones that had been turned over, or where a leaf or two had dropped to the ground. None of it was very clear or very convincing to Walt until some three hours later, he saw half a heel-print. It made his heart race as if he'd been a prospector who had just found a small nugget. Less than an hour later they found her, sitting at the base of tree, whimpering and clutching a rag doll under her chin. She had been missing for two days and Walt doubted if she could have survived another day. Her skin was pale and dry and her eyes distant. When she drank from his canteen he wondered if she was ever going to stop.

When the two returned to the town with the child that night, the posse had also just returned, abandoning their search for the day. The distraught mother was still standing in the street in a state of distress, begging the sheriff to take the men back out in the dark to search.

The child had ridden most of the way back with the Indian, sitting sideways on his lap, as he hummed some sort of chant that soothed the little one. But on getting near the town, he passed her over to Walt. The child made it known that she preferred to stay with the Indian and Walt would have preferred that too, but the old man insisted. When they arrived out of the dark, on walking horses, down the main street of the town, it surprised the crowd assembled outside the sheriff's office.

'Good Lord,' came a shout. 'The child's been saved.'

The mother turned, froze for a second, then collapsed to the ground. What followed was pandemonium and hoopla. Walt was slapped on the back by a score of hands, while the Indian stood off to one side, on his own, and watered his horse from the sheriff's trough. Walt didn't learn much about tracking that day other than it was a fine and clever skill, but he did learn a lot about human nature and not much of it was very appealing. As the years followed they only seemed to confirm that early lesson: that people see only what they want to see, and those who deserve reward rarely get it.

As they continued north, they passed a number of travellers heading southwards and Walt took the time to turn his horse around and ride with them for a short while, just long enough to ask if they had seen a young man travelling on his own. None had.

Later in the day, towards mid-afternoon, the country to their right started to rise into rocky outcrops. Walt kept his eye upon these ragged peaks and brush-covered slopes, and he wondered if Justin Roy had made a random decision to leave the road and head due north, looking for cover. If he had, then he would be impossible to find, at least in the short term. But that was not what Walt suspected the young cowboy would do. He was sure he was going to a place that was familiar, and that he was not on some random search in the hope of finding a hiding-place by chance. Walt felt sure that it was most likely that he was heading for a place he had known since he was a boy.

While he had no first-hand experience of the country around Honey Creek, Walt tried to imagine what might make a favourite spot, one that a family would return to year after year. He figured that it would be a place close to water, most likely a running stream and one that allowed for fishing. It would, he guessed, be sheltered by the woods or by folds in the ground to give protection from the wind, but would not be too difficult to get into or out of. He told himself that it would be pleasant to the eye, and that it would have a place for a safe fire, one that could be left burning while unattended. And, he considered, summer shade from the trees upon the grass to keep the ground cool.

Walt was jogged from these pleasant daydreams of an idyllic camp, when he nearly rode into the other three riders who had stopped.

'This is the main trail into Honey Creek,' said the sheriff from Red Oak. 'It follows the main stream, so we can water the horses as we go. It could get a little steep in parts and we may have to dismount.'

The sheriff looked at Walt as if waiting for a response.

'Sounds fine,' he said, not knowing what else to say. A little worried that he might be caught out for being dozy, he added, 'Lead on.'

29

HIDDEN BEAUTY

The trail ran close to the southern side of a wide shallow stream as they moved east in single file with Walt at the rear. About two miles up from the turn-off, where they had left the road from Red Oak, and half an hour before last light, they made camp on a flat spot under a stand of birch trees.

'This is most pleasant,' said Lawyer Harris.

'Prettier further up at the creek,' was the response from Sheriff Townsend of Red Oak.

'We are in your debt, Sheriff,' said the lawyer. 'Your assistance is invaluable.'

The sheriff responded with a smile and a nodding head. 'I don't want to see the boy harmed and helping Sheriff Ireland is my duty.'

Walt just gave out a low grunt and repeated the word, 'duty', under his breath, before biting into a strip of salted beef.

The agreement struck with Sheriff Townsend was that he would spend one day to assist in the actual search for Justin Roy then return to Red Oak. This would mean that he was away from his town for just over three days, with the day's travel each way to and from Honey Creek, as he said that was all the time he could afford. Walt wanted to press him for at least one more day, as he argued that an extra set of eyes would be most valuable in their search, but Sheriff Ireland wouldn't press the matter and now Lawyer Harris was signing off with his magnanimous praise of Darcy Townsend's assistance, which would put an end to any further discussion. This made Walt as cantankerous as hell, but he bit his tongue.

The next morning they left just after first light and continued up by the stream, crossing to the northern bank. Here the slopes of the small river valley became steeper and were covered on the high ground by ponderosa pines. In the morning sun the dappled light through the leaves of the birch trees sparkled upon the crystal-clear creek, to mesmerize the riders.

In his bones Walt could feel that they were getting close. The country told him so. Not only could you survive with relative ease, but also be content of heart with the surroundings, at least till winter came. It was beautiful country and relaxing on the eye. For the first time in years he felt like he just wanted to pull up, sit down and look, taking in the beauty of the landscape. A pike broke the surface with a loud splash and brought him back to reality.

Two hours on they came to two tributaries flowing in to the creek almost opposite each other, with small trails running alongside, leading up into higher country to both the left and the right.

Walt gave a muffled call for all to stop, then rode up close. 'I think these are worth exploring,' he said, lifting his voice a little over the babble of the water.

The two sheriffs shifted in their saddles to look to the left and right, but didn't seem to have an opinion either way.

'If a man wanted to hide away, then he'd get off the main stream,' explained Walt.

Sheriff Ireland seemed to agree with a twist of his head to one side, but then deferred to the sheriff of Red Oak. 'What you think, Darcy?'

'Suppose,' Darcy said, then looked at Walt. 'I can only give you an hour or two, then I've got to head back.'

'I thought we had a three-day deal,' said Walt.

'That's right. If I leave by midday, I'll be back on the road by nightfall to rest up, then back in Red Oak by tomorrow evening. That makes three days in all.'

Walt mumbled something about people who no longer rode in the dark.

Sheriff Townsend didn't catch his words. 'What was that?'

Walt caught the look on the lawyer's face. 'Nothing,' he replied, but it was said as if by an insolent child.

'So, we go right and you go left,' said Townsend.

'No,' said Walt. 'You two know Roy by his face. The lawyer and me only know him from a photograph we saw back in Bismarck. Best one of us go with each of you.'

Townsend nodded, 'Sure,' he said. 'Any preferences?'

'I'll go with you, Lawyer Harris can go with Sheriff Ireland.' Walt caught the look on the lawyer's face, which indicated that he wasn't sure if the matching-up was right, but Walt wanted to keep the sheriff from Red Oak in the search for as long as possible. 'And I'd like to look up to the left.' Walt really didn't have a preference. He was just being ornery by dictating it, and he knew it. 'And I suggest we meet back here mid-afternoon,' he added.

Sheriff Townsend's head jerked a little. 'I want to be well on my way back down to the road by then.'

Walt pulled his horse to the left and started to cross the shallow creek. 'It's all downhill,' he said. 'So, you'll still be back down at the overnight campsite by this evening.' He didn't look back to get an agreement. He had made a statement of fact and was in no mood for a debate.

The narrow trail alongside the small watercourse turned to the left about a quarter of a mile up, and the rocky sides of the gully became very steep. For the next quarter mile he was concerned that the narrow ravine would come to an end in a waterfall. If it did, then he would know that they had searched up a short blind alley. The sheriff would then tip his hat, turn around and head off back to Red Oak. But just at the narrowest point, where the trail actually entered into the flowing creek, it turned sharp right to expose an open grassy field about 200 yards wide and about twice as long.

'Well, take a look at that,' said Townsend. 'Isn't that something?'

Even Walt had to agree. They both stopped and sat on their mounts side by side to drink in the view.

'Any other places like this in the hills?'

'None that I've ever seen or even been told about. This is a real little hidden beauty.'

As the horses began to walk, Walt kept looking for signs of life; then just up a little, he saw some hoofprints close to the creek bank, which ran down through the small pasture.

The sheriff looked as he pointed them out.

'Cattle,' said Walt.

'Cows,' said the sheriff. He motioned across the low-grassed slope towards the trees to where three milk cows stood, about 250 yards away, idly chewing and looking back at the two men.

'Lost?' questioned Walt.

'I doubt it.'

As Walt searched the tree line, looking for a dwelling, the sound of an axe striking dry wood echoed down from the rise. 'Life,' he said. 'We've got life.'

30

THE MESSAGE

The cabin was back in under the pines, small, squat and neat with a low-pitched earthen roof. A barn of sorts almost adjoined the house, and it too was small with a door just wide enough for single stock to pass through. As they approached the steps of the front veranda a wisp of thin blue smoke drifted low through the pines to the faint smell of burnt coffee.

Walt and Sheriff Townsend dismounted. As they were tying off their horses to the railing, a voice came from behind at the corner of the hut.

'Can I help you folk?'

They both turned to see a Negro man, probably about the same age as Walt, and with silver showing in his hair along with the same colour in the stubble upon his face. However, his height and size, especially the width of his shoulders, showed the strength and shape of a younger man. In his right hand he clenched an axe, his knuckles up close to the head.

'Sheriff Townsend of Red Oak,' came the first introduction.

Walt followed. 'Walt Garfield,' he said and left it at that.

'Moses Carter,' was the reply in a deep, melodic voice.

'You've gone and got yourself a nice place to live, Moses,' said the sheriff.

'Yes sir.' Carter's response was slow, measured and a little reserved.

Walt sensed that they were unwelcome, but his gut didn't tell him that Moses was a man on the run or hiding from the law, until his eyes caught sight of the toe of a rifle butt at the corner of the hut. It had been stood upright, but tucked away, almost out of sight.

'You get many visitors?' asked Walt.

'One or two, but they come in from the other side of the valley. Not many come the way you came. None in winter either way. I get snowed in.'

Walt had to stop himself from a sly grin. *So, you saw which way we came in, didn't you, Moses?* he said to himself.

'You on your own?' asked Sheriff Townsend.

'Yes sir.'

Walt kept his eye on Moses while his mind ran with questions to himself. *If you saw us coming, then you weren't chopping wood out behind your hut.*

'Like it?' continued the sheriff.

'I like it a lot.'

The sheriff looked back down the grassy slop to the end of the valley. 'I can see that.' He then turned back and asked, 'Your land?'

Moses looked uncomfortable. 'No sir, I just came here to squat and this is where I have stayed.' Then he added. 'Until I am moved along.'

'That's not what we are here for,' said Walt and he caught a look of relief in the big man's eyes. 'We are looking for a young man by the name of Justin Roy from Red Oak. Have you seen a cowboy riding around on his own?'

Moses didn't respond straight away. It was as if he was considering the best answer. 'No sir, can't say I have.'

Townsend looked up the slope to the top of the valley where it crested in a line of dark green against the clear sky. 'You get around up there at all?'

'Sure, most days.'

'Seen nothing recent? Any sign on the ground, of horses.'

'None,' then he added, 'sir.' It was said with a hint of disquiet.

'You can get in from that side, you say?' The sheriff was taking an interest in the beauty of the scenery as he looked around.

'That's right.'

'Where does it lead?'

'Down on to the road to Red Oak.'

'Really. How far?'

'Seven or eight mile.'

'Easy ride?'

'Harder coming up, but easy going down, two hours, no more than three.'

'I might just give that a try,' said the sheriff.

Walt kept his eyes on Moses and saw his shoulders drop just a little with a sense of relief as Sheriff Townsend talked of departure.

'You here on your own, Moses?' asked Walt.

The shoulders of the big man instantly tightened again and Walt noticed.

'Yes,' he said slowly. 'Just me.'

'Are you interested why we are searching for this young man from Red Oak, Justin Roy?' asked Walt.

Moses' eyes flashed. 'I don't ask about what is none of my business.'

Walt lifted his head a little, then nodded slowly, as if to show that he accepted the explanation, but he was setting a snare. He believed that if Moses had nothing to hide, then he would say nothing more. To do so would be to justify what didn't need to be justified.

Walt waited, his eyes set in a stare.

The seconds passed.

'I find it best that way,' said the big man.

A voice shouted in Walt's head: *someone is here and I bet it is Justin Roy.* But he knew that he had to play this one cool. If Roy did a runner into these hills he'd never find him.

'The boy is at risk,' said Walt. 'He has a price on his head, but he is not wanted by the law. I'm here with the sheriff to find and protect him from every lowlife proclaimer who wants to get rich quick by killing an innocent man. If you see him will you tell him that?' Walt paused, then said. 'Tell him that Walter Garfield has been sent to protect him.'

The big man looked straight at Walt. 'I got that, Mr Garfield and if I see him I'll pass on your message.'

'Thank you, Moses, I would be obliged.'

Walt waited for Moses to ask how Justin Roy could get in touch with him, should he get to pass the message, but he didn't.

Townsend pulled himself back on to his mount. 'I'm done here,' he said, looking up the valley. 'I'm going to head back to Red Oak and try that route over the ridge.'

Walt mounted. 'I'll ride with you,' he said, then quickly turned his horse and stepped it up close to the sheriff in an effort to shield any comment he might make about returning to

Red Oak on his own and leaving Walt in the hills. But the sheriff just gave a nod towards Moses, then turned his horse away from the cabin and towards the high ground.

Walt gave a small wave in parting, as a gesture of goodwill. Moses gave a small wave in return, but it came with no other response. As the two rode towards the ridge Walt debated in his mind if he should confide in the sheriff his belief that Justin Roy was back at the cabin, probably hiding behind the hut, where he had been chopping wood. But as they reached the top of the ridge and the vista opened wide before them to show the ground falling away down to where the road to Red Oak lay, the sheriff turned to him with a smile.

'Well, it's all yours now,' he said, as he tapped two upright fingers against the brim of his hat.

'Yeah, I guess it is,' said Walt without offering his hand.

Townsend turned his horse and kicked his heels without looking back.

Their short relationship had been poor from the start and in a quieter moment, Walt might have conceded that he could have contributed to its fragility. But at that precise moment he was incensed by the rapid departure of the sheriff as he watched him ride off down the far side of the ridge at full tilt. He grabbed at the brim of his hat, pulled it from his head in a flurry and swooped it down against his leg, to strike in a blur of dust.

'Geez!' The word hissed through clenched teeth as he gave a wild shake of his head. 'Geezas.' He sucked in a breath, then, agitated and annoyed, he rolled out of the saddle to relieve himself. When his feet struck the ground he kicked at a small rock, but his timing was way out: it rolled under the toe of his boot and down to the heel to unexpectedly throw him off balance. His right leg kicked up into the air and as his weight shifted to his left leg, his knee buckled and down he came upon his backside with a thump.

'Damn and geezas,' he yelled as his horse stepped back out of the way and neighed. 'Don't you start mocking,' he yelled from his prostrate position. His horse lifted its head then dropped it down close to Walt's face as if to examine the curious sight. 'Seen enough?' asked Walt, crossly.

Slowly he stood upright, then reached back down to pick up his hat from the dirt. He saw the offending rock lying there and went to kick at it for a second time, just as his horse neighed again. He stopped, thinking it better to leave the damn thing alone, and placed his hat on his head, but not quite straight, before he sniffed and spat to one side, undid his belt and started to relieve himself against a small bush.

Just after he had pulled himself back into the saddle and was about to turn his horse towards the hut, he drew his canteen to his mouth. The water seemed to cool his jangled nerves; then just as he was screwing the lid back into place he heard the shot. It came from down on the far side of the ridge, where the sheriff had disappeared on his ride back to the road to Red Oak. It had come from probably a quarter-mile off, no more. It was just a single shot and Walt guessed that it was a rifle shot.

He swung his horse around to face towards where the report had come from, but could see nothing. There was no sign of any activity, no dust, no smoke, nothing. Maybe, he concluded, the errant sheriff had just taken the opportunity to put a jackrabbit into the dinner pot. But he dismissed such a notion as a fancy, since the sheriff had shown that he was not keen on delaying his return to Red Oak. Then he heard a second shot, which echoed with a crack through the still air. Walt froze with concern, his body bolt upright. Another crack, a third shot, and then a moment later half a dozen staccato shots followed. 'Oh, Geezas,' he said aloud, 'ambush.' He booted his horse into life.

31

SIN

Walt rode at a gallop in a beeline straight for where he had seen the sheriff just minutes before. About half a mile down the slope, as he approached the tree line, he slowed to a trot and put his hand to the grip of his Colt. It was an instinctive reaction to reassure and check that his handgun was ready when needed. Near a stand of red oaks he picked up an old trail, just wide enough for one horse. Upon this path he could clearly see the broken ground from the galloping hoofs of the sheriff's horse, whicht had just passed.

He slowed his horse to a walk and leaned forward with his head low and to the left of the mane, straining to catch sight of anyone ahead. Then just below, out of the corner of his eye, he glimpsed a splash of blood upon the ground. It passed under the hoofs of his horse so quickly that he wondered if he had mistaken some naturally occurring stain. Then he saw another, just to the front, an elongated splash of red, so he brought his horse to a halt.

Walt eased up to sit taller and slowly twisted from side to side, searching to the left and right of the trail, but he saw nothing. He slowly drew his .45 from its holster and held the muzzle upright as he pulled back on the hammer.

Then, to the left and through the trees, he caught sight of three horsemen nearly 100 yards off, riding parallel to the trail and up towards the ridge at no more than a walking pace. It was plain that they hadn't seen him, as their departure was orderly and in no haste, but he had no doubt that these were the men who had fired their arms.

Walt sat still with just his eyes following their silhouettes as they disappeared through the foliage. He then slowly edged his horse forward down the trail, his urgency directed towards finding the sheriff, but as he moved he kept low, glancing back to make sure that he hadn't been sighted.

Nearly 200 yards on and to the right of the trail he saw the sheriff's horse. It lay on its side with a hind leg sticking out across the track and trembling, but life had all but gone. As he drew up alongside the animal he could see a number of wounds to the stomach and neck, but the lethal blows had been two shots to the head. One was near the ear and the other was just below the left eye. Each wound now leaked blood, which was pooling upon the hard ground of the trail.

Walt eased down out of the saddle, his pistol held upright in one hand, the reins clasped tight in the other. He looked around, turning slowly in a complete circle expecting at any moment to hear a shot, while he searched for Sheriff Townsend, but he could see nothing. He looked down in swift glances for any sign, marks, tracks, or a blood trail. Then his eyes caught sight of a boot, empty but still ensnared in the right stirrup, which had been flicked up over the saddle when the horse had fallen.

Walt pulled on the reins and turned his horse back down the trail, then slowly began to walk back, constantly looking out to the right where he had seen the riders departing from this scene. Thirty yards along and to his right, and about ten yards from the trail, was what looked like a small pile of discarded clothing. But Walt knew what it was; he'd seen similar clumps as a young soldier. It was the twisted lifeless body of the fallen. It was the sheriff of Red Oak, Darcy Townsend.

Marks leading to the body clearly showed where he had come off his horse, then been dragged through the leaves to this final spot by his attackers. As Walt approached he could see the sheriff's feet. On one foot was a boot while on the other was a cotton sock with a small hole on the back of the heel.

Walt walked three paces past the body, then turned his horse around to face back towards the trail. If he needed to escape he would ride straight out on to the trail, turn south and ride like hell. But only far enough to break from any fire and find a suitable place to dismount, draw his Winchester, and engage his pursuers.

He leant in over the sheriff, who was lying face down with his jacket pulled up over his head. Two wounds showed on his back, and as Walt lifted the coat away to view the face, he saw a bullet wound to the forehead, fired close up, showing black powder marks around the wound.

The sight sparked a flash of anger in Walt's gut. 'You sons of bitches.' The words came from his lips with venom. 'You shoot first, then figure out if you got the right man. Only to kill off the evidence when you find you haven't.' He turned his face away and spat, then wiped his sleeve across his mouth while still holding his Colt, and cursed. 'I swear, if I ever get the chance. . . .' At that moment, kneeling beside the still warm body of an officer of the law, Walt swore a silent oath that he would bring to account those who had played any part in this sin, and that included the powerful and wealthy industrialist, Richard Tambling.

32

REAPER

Walt holstered his Colt and knelt on one knee alongside the dead sheriff, while still facing in the direction where he had last seen the three horsemen. He pulled the lawman's jacket back down from where it had bunched around the shoulders, then rolled the body over. His fingers unclipped the star from near the lapel, and then undid the buckle on the gunbelt, pulling it free. He quickly felt the pockets for anything of importance, an old habit from long ago when letters, neatly written and folded for such an occasion, were carried into battle. There were none. The sheriff had not prepared for the possibility of death this day.

Walt's final act was to place each arm across the chest as if ready for wrapping and burial; but as he went to stand, he paused, then patted the sheriff's shoulder, twice. It was a small and simple gesture of compassion and a silent admission that he had once again been impetuous in his dealings with others. He had let the sheriff annoy and anger him, but at that very particular moment he couldn't remember, for the life of him, why.

When he mounted his horse, after placing the sheriff's rig and star into the left side of his saddle valise, he pulled his Winchester from its leather scabbard and checked the action before returning it to its sheath. He then took a drink of water from his canteen, swished the last mouthful over his tongue then spat it out to the side away from the sheriff's body. He walked his horse back to the narrow trail and turned right to head back to Moses' hut. Exactly what route he should take, he didn't know, other than it must be one that kept him out of sight. Walt's mind now began to race, weighing up what he needed to do. One thing remained clear – he had to find Justin Roy and he had to find him fast, real fast. Just how he would then protect the young man, well, he'd have to figure that out later, not now, he told himself. He recalled the words of his old platoon sergeant, who had repeated throughout the war to his young soldiers: *First things first, always keep first things first.* And now was not the time to get too far ahead.

So first, he would retrace his steps back up the narrow trail to where it came out on to the open ground that led to the top of the ridge; from there he would decide on a route over the ridge and back to the hut. As he rode, at no more than a walking pace, upright and alert, he kept constantly touching his pistol and glancing at his rifle. It was a nervous thing, like a twitch of the eye that couldn't be helped, and Walt knew that it was a sign of an old man who was becoming cautious.

Just before he got to the end of the path, where it emerged from the woods and on to the open grassland, he stopped and leant back to pull the sheriff's handgun from the leather valise. Why? He wasn't sure, other than for having the comfort of another handgun, yet his Colt had never failed him in the past. As he went to pull the gun free from the holster, while it was still in the saddle-bag the rig twisted and jammed the weapon in tight; so, with a silent curse, he dismounted to pull it free.

The gun was a Remington single action Army with hard black rubber grips and a small securing ring on the base of the butt. Its solid feel and balance were pleasing to the hand and for a second or two Walt pondered whether it was time to update his old Colt. Suddenly the crack of a dry branch off to the right jerked him back from his thoughts. He looked up over his horse's rump to see a small group of men some fifty yards off, on rising ground. Had he not stopped, he would have missed them completely, as their horses were turned away so that he was looking at their rear ends; the three riders had been crouching just off to one side. As they now started to stand, one bent forward and brushed dirt from his knees.

A mixed feeling of alarm and relief swept over Walt. He was outnumbered, outgunned and in no position to escape. If they turned and looked his way they would see him, but he had seen them first. So at that moment he held the upper hand. He carefully pushed the sheriff's pistol into the waistband of his trousers then slowly reached forward and pulled his Winchester from its scabbard, whispering to his horse to stay steady before he gently tied off the reins to a near sapling.

A clear shot through the woods would not be possible; he would have to advance closer to ensure a single shot kill. Walt drew in a deep breath then went into a slight crouch as he brought the rifle to the shoulder letting the muzzle drop a little, so that he could get a clear view over the weapon and at his targets. As he began to advance, ever so carefully, he kept his gaze upon the three men and was therefore unable to look down at his feet, so each step was taken with concentrated caution. When he moved each foot forward he did so slowly, while ensuring that his stationary leg was able to maintain his weight and balance. When he placed each foot upon the ground, he eased the outside of the boot down first then rolled it into position, holding his breath in the hope that any noise would not carry.

As Walt advanced, a little like a cat stalking prey, he constantly considered in what order he would engage the three targets. His first shot would be fired at the target that offered the best clear view and the biggest area at which to aim. But while that first single shot would surprise, it would only do so for a fleeting moment.

Walt knew that when fired upon men instantly and instinctively turned their heads towards the sound. But this first response lasts for no more than a split second before they immediately seek cover, mostly by throwing themselves to the ground. Once down, lying prone and facing the threat, the odds of their survival are greatly enhanced, but at a price. Down low, especially in woodland, is a poor position from which to identify a target and retaliate, other than with wild shots in the general direction.

A composed man, one of experience and strong nerves, will go down on to one knee, reducing his target size, to adopt a firing position from which to return accurate fire back at his attacker. But composure is a rare quality in a gunfight. The instinct for survival is deeply ingrained in every man and it takes over involuntarily. For some, the ear-splitting noise, along with the chaos and confusion, all laced with immediate and close danger is just too much to bear and they take little part in the battle. When that happens they are no longer protecting themselves with fire, just depending on divine providence to save their skin.

Walt was now within thirty yards of his quarry, but he still had no clear line of sight to any of the three targets. The men remained obscured by their horses and preoccupied, when the sound of laughter cut through the air followed by a whoop and holler. Walt stopped perfectly still, watching as one waved his arms about as if he were acting upon a stage. Then, another, the one on the right, a solid man in a long dark coat, turned towards Walt and with his head down began to advance straight towards him.

Walt lifted the muzzle of his Winchester and sighted on the centre of the man's chest as he kept walking closer, closer, each step closer, until he stopped less than fifteen yards away in a small clearing. He opened his coat, undid his trousers, pulled himself free and began to relieve himself, his head still downcast, his hat covering most of his face.

Walt held his aim, his finger upon the smooth curved trigger, his breathing slow and even, his sighting-mark firm and steady as he watched the brim of the hat slowly start to lift to expose the lips, then the nose, and last of all the eyes.

Walt knew the face immediately. It was Jude Radford from Tennessee, who he had seen in Bismark with Pat Harrison and Lenny Griffiths. Each man looked at the other. For that moment Radford's eyes seemed to expand to twice their size. 'Oh, no,' came the quivering mumble from his lips as he fumbled for his gun, just as Walt squeezed the trigger.

The shot exploded from the muzzle and punched into Radford's chest with a thud, collapsing him to his knees. His head then slowly pitched forward, still wearing his hat as the crown struck the base of a small tree, so that he was now bent forward as if preparing to stand on his head.

Walt didn't see any of this. He had lifted his head and run forward ten paces, working the lever action on the Winchester to reload for the second shot while still keeping the weapon to his shoulder. He was looking for a clear line to the other two targets, who had now gone to ground. One had gone right, the other left, as their horses turned and stomped their hoofs, cracking the brush and obscuring his view.

A shot was fired in return and Walt heard the bullet pass through the foliage, just off to his left and above head height, but no more than a yard or two away, sending small leaves falling to the ground. But he held his fire. He wanted a target, so he moved to the right, two paces, searching for a clear line, just as he caught a glimpse of a shape as it sought cover behind a horse.

Walt ran forward another five or six paces as a second shot fired, to strike the ground in front of him to his left, no more than a pace away, to kick up dirt and shower it against the side of his leg. He went down on one knee and turned to where the shot had been fired, just as a riderless horse broke free to race off to the left. It was followed by a yell from the right to signal that one of the riders had mounted and was now urging his horse to escape.

Walt stood and took a snap shot at the departing target but missed, firing too high, just as a return round struck the tree next to him at head height. He swivelled to the left and fired three rapid shots in the direction from where he believed the shot had come. He saw a crouching figure start to make its getaway on foot. Walt steadied, took aim at the moving target, but before he could fire another shot rang out and the figure dropped to the ground.

Walt was momentarily confused and wondered if there was another shooter in the woods, one he had not seen who had now entered the battle on his side. But he pushed this notion from his mind; he knew he was on his own and that he had to advance and close with this last target or lose the opportunity. With his rifle still to his shoulder, he began to walk forward with deliberate steps while sweeping the barrel of his Winchester through an arc, searching from left to right. Then, twenty-five paces forward he saw Lenny Griffiths, also from Tennessee, propped up on one elbow, hands held up, palms facing out to show that he had given up. His upper left leg was locked straight and bloodied along its length from the top of the thigh down past the side of the knee and into the calf. It was an odd wound as the bullet had cut the trouser leg open lengthways, to expose the extent of the deep elongated injury.

Walt stopped, a little out of breath and stood over the casualty. 'Well, well, Lenny,' he said. 'I guess I got lucky with one of my wild shots.'

'No, I got unlucky,' came the response. 'I shot myself by mistake as I was running for cover.'

'Is that so?' Walt lowered his Winchester to reveal a grin as he examined the injury. 'Bad wound. You've opened that leg right up. Seen men lose a limb for less.'

'Need help.' It was an appeal for compassion.

Walt crouched down and took a closer look. 'I would think you do.' He kept peering with interest as he asked, 'Who got away?'

'Pat.'

'Harrison?' Walt kept examining the wound.

Griffiths nodded.

'Well I'll be. His luck is still holding after all these years. I thought he would have used up all of his nine lives long before now.'

'He's blessed like you, Reaper.'

Walt turned his head and spat on the ground. 'Now that's a name I haven't heard for some time. Certainly not since I left the marshal service, and parted company with lowlife like you, Lenny.'

'You no longer wearing a badge?'

'Nope. All hung up.'

'We didn't know you were no longer practising. We saw you in Bismarck and just thought you were still with the law. We cleared out in case you had some warrants.'

'You need to keep up with times then,' said Walt, 'cos I'm a mister now.'

'If Pat had known—' Lenny stopped and his head seemed to quiver before he coughed, then he drew in a quick breath, 'That it was you shooting at him, on your own, he would have stayed and had it out.'

'Why so?'

'You killing his brother and all.'

'I killed two of his brothers.'

'His step-brother don't count to Pat. He never got on with him, but with Garth it was different. They were close.'

'If he was so keen to settle up why didn't he do it in Bismarck?'

'He had a clear eye on the reward. Said it would be our recompense, our last chance and that scores could be settled later. And he said they would.'

'Ahhh, money before honour, that's Pat Harrison all right.'

'So are you after the reward too, now that you ain't marshalling any more? Are you chasing Roy as well?'

'Reward? Nope, not me. I'm the one who's been sent to keep him safe.'

Lenny was turning pale and his breathing was becoming laboured. 'Hope you're getting paid well, cos you got a lot of competition coming after you. The blacksmith in Red Oak is selling advice, for twenty-five dollars apiece, that Roy is up in these hills. We just happened to get here first.'

'Yeah, you got here first and killed a sheriff.'

'That was just a mistake. He came on us real quick and we thought it was Roy trying to escape.'

'Yeah, I saw the powder burns of that mistake on his forehead.'

Lenny looked away. 'That was Pat, I didn't want no part of that.' He then looked back at Walt. 'I swear to God.' It was a plaintive plea.

'Is that a fact?' said Walt as he transferred his Winchester from his right to left hand, then reached down and pulled the sheriff's Remington from his trouser band. Lenny looked concerned as Walt pulled back on the hammer, then leant forward and placed the muzzle of the revolver between Lenny's eyes. 'Well, you discuss your oath with the good Lord when you see him and give him my regards,' said Walt. Then he squeezed on the trigger.

33

PERSUASIVE

Only ninety minutes had passed from the the sheriff's riding off from the top of the ridge to the time when Walt now passed back near that same spot, on his way to Moses' cabin. Yet in that short period three men had died and one, Pat Harrison, was close by with killing on his mind. This turn of events was certainly unexpected but not unsettling, as it was a situation with which Walt was familiar.

He had last killed in '95, some four years previously. That had been his twenty-third killing in the line of duty. Most of those other deaths had come from fair fights, especially in the early years before he was wounded at close quarters in the left buttock. That incident, apart from the pain, inconvenience, and concern that the wound might turn septic – not to mention the embarrassment – had led him to be more prudent in his arrests.

Some comic in the service came up with the nickname of lead arse, which Walt found distasteful as it also gave the impression that he sat around on his backside all day. But luckily that dub turned out to be short lived, when an experienced marshal by the name of Vernon Gibbs took him to one side, saying that he had seen the report into the shooting, and that Walt had been too brave for his own good.

'Seth Howard wasn't aiming to shoot you in the arse. He wanted to shoot you dead,' said the old lawman. 'Take my advice and never give a lowlife that opportunity again. If they are outside the law, shoot first and live to do the paperwork after.'

Walt took the guidance to heart and when sent to serve warrants and arrest a dozen felons in hiding, he ended with nine men killed in six months. Three of them were hardened criminals who had killed law officers and avoided capture for years. The others were well on the way to becoming hardcases, so Walt chose not to give them half a chance.

Walt had reached this score when there came a newspaper article out of Kansas City that a clean-out of villainy had occurred in the Territories, which had seen a number of known assassins dispatched as if by the grim reaper himself. This same title had been attached to him once before by a New York newspaper man named William Lundy, who had accompanied Walt on his first assignment as a deputy marshal, however this time it stuck: Reaper Garfield. He would have preferred to do without it, but he had to agree it was certainly better than Lead Arse Garfield.

As Walt made his way down towards Moses' hut he weighed up the odds that he faced. Had it only been Harrison whom he needed to worry about then he would have been a happy man. A one-on-one fight was even money; he knew Harrison well and recognized what he was capable of. But it was Lenny's news that more proclaimers were on their way that was now of a most pressing concern. When the hordes did eventually arrive in these woods life would not be safe for man nor beast, as trigger-happy vigilantes with the smell of money in their nostrils would shoot at anything that moved.

Walt stayed just inside the tree line as he rode his horse slowly. When he picked up sight of the side of Moses' barn, he was about 150 yards away. The two small buildings were tucked back amongst the trees, and had it not been for the odd wisps of blue smoke there would have been no sign of life in the small valley at all. This provided a degree of security, but eventually a pro-claimer would find it and make his presence known.

Walt picked his way through the pines to come out near the solid corner posts and heavy roofing beams of the barn. As he turned his horse around the corner of the barn he almost ran into Moses, who was standing by the open barn door with a Winchester aimed at Walt's chest.

Walt stopped and splayed his palms to show that he was not handling a weapon. 'It's me, Walt Garfield,' he said.

Moses kept his rifle aimed. 'I heard shooting.'

'Sheriff Townsend was gunned down just over the ridge.'

The big man's face showed immediate concern. 'Who by?'

'Three Tennessee boys.'

'Why?'

'One said that they thought he was Justin Roy trying to escape.'

Moses eyes flashed.

'He also said that more are coming up from Red Oak to join in the hunt. Seems the local blacksmith is selling the word that your boy is up here.'

Moses did not respond to the bait. 'Where are the men who killed the sheriff?'

'Two dead, one escaped.'

'You kill them?'

'Yes, I killed them,' said Walt as he eased out of the saddle. 'Can I water my horse?'

Moses seemed lost as to what to do, then slowly lowered the barrel of his rifle, turned and started to walk towards the hut. Walt followed until they were close to the veranda.

'Water barrel 'tis around the far side.'

Walt nodded and walked past Moses, leading his horse, but as he got to the corner of the cabin he glanced back to see Moses duck up the far side of the building and out of view. As his horse drank he undid the cinch around the girth and ran his hand down over each leg, checking with a squeeze to ensure there was no soreness that might hinder any long hard ride that might lie ahead.

While leaning down, with his hand close to a hoof, he looked along the length of the log wall and sighted the slightest of movements upon the ground. It was the tip of a boot toe, just protruding, no more than an inch or two.

Had it remained stationary Walt doubted if he would have noticed it, as its colour was dark like the stones upon which it stood. But its owner had shifted his weight just a little and Walt's eye had picked up that slight movement. His gut told him that it was Justin Roy.

'Your mother told me where to come to look for you,' he called to the toe of the boot. 'She is worried.'

He received no response, but Walt saw the toe move again, slightly.

'Sheriff Townsend is dead. The men who shot him down thought he was you, and there are more to follow. I've been sent to keep you safe, but I can only do that with your cooperation.'

'Who sent you to keep me safe?' asked the voice of the unseen owner of the boot.

'A lawyer from Pennsylvania by the name of Harris. He and Sheriff Ireland of Bismarck County rode up here with me and the sheriff of Red Oak to find and protect you.'

'Where are the sheriff and lawyer now?'

'Probably waiting for me down by the main creek at the moment.'

The young man stepped out into the open, but Walt didn't immediately look at him.

'What is Sheriff Ireland doing here?'

Walt drew his hand back up his horse's front leg, then looked

113

at the young man. 'He, like the lawyer, me, and your mother, don't want any harm to come to you.'

'Why?'

It seemed like a dopey question to Walt and it showed when he spoke. 'Well, the sheriff wants to uphold the law, the lawyer wants to see justice done, and I guess your mother loves you. What the hell do you think?'

'And you?'

It was an unexpected question and Walt thought about it for a moment as he ran his hand up his horse's neck towards the bridle.

'Me?' he said. 'Well, my reasons are far less righteous. I need the money. If I keep you alive then I get paid by the lawyer.' Walt looked over at the boy, who was standing with his feet together as if at attention. He was a tall, lean young man in dark trousers and wearing a green waistcoat. In his right hand he held a Winchester.

'Mind you,' continued Walt. 'If I was to shoot you dead and claim the reward on your head, I'd be paid handsomely and save myself a lot of trouble.' Walt started to grin as he thought of what he had just said.

Justin Roy didn't, he just looked stern. 'I was found not guilty by a jury in a court of law.'

'I heard that,' said Walt.

'So why has a reward been placed on me?'

Walt turned his head towards his horse while he thought for a second or two, then he looked back towards Roy.

'I don't rightly know the answer to that. Maybe it's the revenge of a father. Or maybe it's anger at the loss of a son. Or maybe it's a crazy old man with far too much money? But as I said, I don't truly know and to be honest, it doesn't really matter at the moment. The reward has been set and you are the target.'

The young man's shoulders slumped. 'I should go and hide.'

'And where are you planning on doing that?'

'I know these hills. I know places.' There was a touch of defiance in his voice.

'So you hide. It still won't change anything. You'll still be a walking target. You can't hide all your life.'

Moses stepped out from behind the cabin to stand behind Justin Roy. 'I will protect him.' In his hand he held an axe.

Walt rubbed his hand across his chin, then spat on the ground. 'Ah geezas,' he said. 'Well, that should work out real fine then.' The derision was clear in his voice.

The boy came to Moses' defence. 'Uncle Moses was a soldier. Fought in the war. Has a medal.'

'A medal? Well, that should help.'

The comment seemed to infuriate the young cowboy.

'What do you suggest Mr Garfield?' came Moses' deep voice.

'I suggest that we all saddle up then head back down to the main creek to join up with Sheriff Ireland and Lawyer Harris.'

'And then?'

'And then I take your boy all the way to Pennsylvania.'

'Why will he be safe in Pennsylvania and not some place else, closer?'

'He won't be any safer in Pennsylvania than he will be in any other place. But it is in Pennsylvania that the proclamation was posted and it's in Pennsylvania that we need to have it rescinded.' Walt looked directly at Justin Roy. 'Until then a ten thousand-dollar reward can be claimed on the basis of a photograph of you lying dead and naked to show off all the bullet holes. Until the offer of that reward is removed, you will continue to walk around with a target glued to the front and back of your shirt. So that's why you need to go to Pennsylvania.'

'But what can I do when I get there, to have the reward lifted?'

'You speak to the father of the man you killed.'

The young man shuffled uneasily on the spot. 'What makes you think that there is anything I can say that will make him change his mind.'

'Probably nothing.'

'So what is the use of going then?' asked Moses.

Walt now got a little irritated. 'Well, maybe because I can't think of any other way.' He then took a breath and softened his tone. 'Or maybe it's easy to have a man killed when you have never met him; but not so easy when you have to look him in the eye and still tell him that you plan to have him executed. Besides,' said Walt, 'there are some things I would like to discuss with him as well, and I am known,' Walt pulled on his trousers to hitch them up a little, 'to be a very persuasive man.'

34

IT WORKS

Walt's idea of going to Pennsylvania to confront Richard Tambling was half-baked and he knew it, but he just couldn't figure out any other way to resolve the situation. That he could get access to Tambling via Lawyer Harris seemed to make some sense of such a stunt, at least in his mind, but the details of any plan were sketchy, very sketchy indeed. He knew that it would be too dangerous to head back south or east towards Red Oak where they had left their horses, as he would run into pro-claimers heading for the hills to lynch Roy. Therefore, it seemed that the best chance was to head west and into Nebraska. If he could make it to Omaha, he could travel by train to Chicago and on to Pennsylvania. Once aboard the train, on a first class ticket, he would lock Roy in his compartment and relax. Then, he told himself, he could discuss the detail with the lawyer, on a col-league-to-colleague basis, about the best way to tackle Tambling.

As Justin Roy packed up his few belongings, Moses acted like a caring uncle, helping to wrap his bedroll and secure his personal items. He then made it known that he would like to ride along with them, at least as far as the creek, to meet up with Lawyer Harris and Sheriff Ireland.

'Is that OK with you?' Moses asked.

'That is exactly what I want you to do. And I don't mind if you come all the way to Pennsylvania with us,' said Walt. 'I can use an extra gun and besides, I'm damned if I'd stay around here and get shot at.'

Moses looked concerned. 'Why would I be shot at?'

'The lowlifes who are interested in making a claim on your boy are willing to shoot at anyone, and then ask for a name. So it could be a simple case of mistaken identity.'

Moses looked down at the back of his hand. 'I don't know how?'

Walt thought about it for a little. 'You should be OK during the day, but I wouldn't venture out in the dark.'

'Only a fool would mistake me for a young white boy. I'll be fine,' said Moses.

Roy turned to Walt. 'Will Moses be fine, Mr Garfield?'

'Walt. It's Walt,' Walt said. He looked across at Moses. 'You ever had trouble up here before?'

'No. I don't see many folk and none in winter.'

'Well, you'll have someone knocking on your door this time and if they get wind that you were protecting their prize, well, I don't know. All of them have records and most have killed for no good reason. If they think you have information they will get it out of you, one way or another. None of the proclaimers I saw in the Bismarck county hall respect anything, and least of all—' Walt cut himself short.

Moses finished for him. 'Least of all a Nigra?'

Walt paused before he said. 'Yeah,' then added. 'But it's nothing personal.'

Moses pulled a face. 'And how do you figure that?'

'They hate Indians, Mexican, Chinese, bankers and lawyers

just as much as they hate you. On par, choosing between the two of us, I think most would shoot me first.'

'Sounds like I'm in good company then.'

Walt recognized the good humour and smiled. 'Yeah, I've met good and bad in each of those folk I've just named, and until recently I would have put lawyers at the top of the list. But Lawyer Harris is proving me wrong.' Then he added, 'So far.'

Justin Roy now looked very concerned. 'Maybe you should come along with us, Moses, at least until this blows over.'

'You good with a gun?' asked Walt.

Roy answered for him, declaring. 'He is a decorated soldier.'

Walt was unimpressed. 'Not all soldiers are good with guns. Even the decorated ones who got a medal for counting beans.'

'He was not—'

Moses cut him short. 'I can shoot,' he said.

'What do you carry?'

'I used to carry a .44 Colt 1860 Army. No need now, but I still keep it clean and oiled.'

Walt had to stop from saying, *have you got any ammunition for that antique?* but instead he simply asked. 'Caps?'

'Of course.'

'You never bothered to upgraded to cartridges?'

'No need to. I only ever use a shotgun now days.'

'What type?'

'I got two. The best is a Stevens 10 gauge.'

'One or two barrels?'

'Double.'

'Now that could come in real handy, so bring that along too,' said Walt. He switched his gaze on to the young man. 'And where's your rig?'

'I don't carry a handgun any more. Just a rifle for hunting.' It was said in a pious voice.

'Oh. And why is that?' asked Walt.

'It did me no good. I killed a man and nearly ended up in jail or worse, so I decided that from then on I'd stay away from handguns.' It was said as a rehearsed declaration, the sort of thing pronounced in a tent or down by the river just before a baptism.

'How noble,' mumbled Walt sarcastically.

'What was that?' asked Roy.

Walt left the small cabin without answering. He returned with Sheriff Townsend's rig in his hand and threw it towards the young man.

Roy caught it and looked down at the belt with the handgun in its polished tan leather holster and the loops that held gleaming cartridges. 'I don't want it,' he said.

'It's near new and belonged to Sheriff Townsend.'

'I don't care, I don't want it.'

Walt drew in a breath and his face took on that look; the one that says *I don't need this right now.*

'Well, let me tell you something, *Mister-I've-Declared-To-Stay-Away-From-Handguns.* That's the rig a lawman was carrying when he came to find and protect you. He was gunned down before he could pull it from the holster to defend himself. The reprobates that shot him down thought it was you, then when they realized their mistake they knew that there was no going back, so they shot him dead in cold blood. Now strap that on to your thigh and be prepared to use it to protect your hide.'

Justin Roy looked at Moses.

Moses nodded his approval.

Roy slowly started to put the belt around his hips.

'You'll need to replace one of the cartridges,' said Walt. 'I tested it for you and it works.'

35

PENNSYLVANIA BOUND

The ride back down to Honey Creek was done just inside the pines and close to the north side of the small valley. Moses led the way, followed by Justin Roy then Walt. The old soldier had strapped on his old Army Colt and was resting his Stevens 10-gauge across his lap, while holding it steady with his right hand. The big man sat straight-backed and rode with a light touch as he weaved his horse through the trees, stopping from time to time, but always indicating first with a low hand signal. Walt had to concede that yes, Moses had seen field service and was now quickly falling back into familiar ways.

Close to three hours had passed since Sheriff Townsend and Walt had parted on top of the ridge, and nearly five hours since the two of them had left the company of Lawyer Harris and Sheriff Ireland. Walt was now concerned that his delay in getting back would cause the sheriff and lawyer to come looking along the tributary that he and Sheriff Townsend had taken. If they had not heard the shooting on the other side of the ridge they could, unawares, easily ride into the open valley to present a target to Pat Harrison, who would be on edge and trigger-happy. If that happened Walt knew that he would have no other choice but to ride out into the open and intercept them before they ran for cover. To lose them before last light would cause precious time to be lost: time that could be vital to their chances of escape. So he told Moses of his intentions should that occur, adding that he should continue to escort Roy out of the valley and down to the tributary junction, where they would then meet up.

Moses answered with a crisp, 'Yes sir.'

Gee, thought Walt, I could have done with such an obliging attitude in some of my deputies.

When they got to the end of the valley and to where the small tributary flowed into the narrow gorge, Walt voiced his concern that the sheriff and the lawyer might already have entered the valley.

'No one has passed this way since you and Sheriff Ireland,' said Moses.

'You sure?' asked Walt; showing his scepticism.

'You don't believe me?' asked Moses.

Justin Roy added, 'He was—'

Walt cut in. 'I know: he was in the Army, but not everybody in the Army can read sign, and that includes me.'

'Moses can,' said Roy with defiance. 'Indians taught him.'

Walt seemed inclined to dismiss this information, but he looked over at Moses. 'Are you sure? No sign?'

'I'm sure,' said Moses.

'OK, let's get on to the creek and I'll lead, I know the way from here. And I want them to see it's me, not some someone who they think is a proclaimer.'

When they arrived at the intersection of the two tributaries that led into the main creek there was no sign of the sheriff or the lawyer.

Moses bent forward in the saddle to examine the ground. 'Been a bit of coming and going through here,' he said.

'Yeah, four of us came through here mid-morning.' Walt told him,

'This looks later. Lots of sign.'

'There were four of us,' repeated Walt.

'This is more than four horses and it's recent.'

'Let me see.' Walt rode up alongside Moses and bent forward

to look at the mass of hoofprints on the bank of the creek. 'How many?' he asked.

'Well, three or four riders have gone up there.' Moses pointed to the tributary where Sheriff Ireland and the Lawyer Harris had gone to explore.

'There were only two,' said Walt.

Moses moved his horse forward a pace and pointed. 'The same have gone up, down and up again.'

'What?'

'Same horses. You can tell by the shoes. The others over there are different. They continued up Honey.'

Walt could see a large number of hoofprints, but guessed that Harris and Ireland had come back down the tributary, then gone for a look along Honey Creek. He was thinking of drawing his pistol and firing a signal shot when Roy asked,

'Why don't you believe Moses?'

'I didn't say I didn't.'

'But you doubt him?'

'I'm a born doubter,' declared Walt.

'Moses said the riders who went up the small creek are different from the ones that went up the big creek.'

'Well, thank you for the clarification,' said Walt through tight lips.

'He's just saying your people are still up there.' Justin Roy indicated up the tributary with a glance. 'And that a different group continued up Honey Creek.'

'Yeah, I got all that,' said Walt, but there was still disbelief in his voice.

'If you want to find Sheriff Ireland we need to go up there.' Roy pointed this time, just to reinforce where they had to go.

Walt wasn't convinced, but if by chance Moses was right and there were other riders searching along Honey Creek he didn't want to alert them with a shot.

'I'll lead,' he said.

'I'll follow up last,' said Moses.

As Walt rode past Justin Roy, he got a condemning glance.

'Don't start,' he said, and kicked his heels back to speed up his departure.

They hadn't gone more than a hundred yards before Walt sighted Sheriff Ireland, who was squatting close to the bank with his Winchester to his shoulder. He gave a wave to acknowledge that he had seen Walt, then stood up.

Walt signalled back, dismounted and walked the last twenty paces to where the sheriff waited.

'I thought for a moment you were unwanted company,' said the sheriff.

'Where's the lawyer?' asked Walt.

Sheriff Ireland put a finger to his lips to send the message for him to speak softly. 'Back up a little with the horses.'

Walt lowered his voice. 'You've had company?'

'We ran into a little trouble out on the creek, so we ducked back up here to hide.'

'What sort of trouble?'

'Shooting trouble. Did you not hear?'

Walt looked concerned. 'No. You both OK?'

'Fine, but I think it scared the pants off the lawyer,' said the sheriff as he rubbed his left temple. He looked over Walt's shoulder. 'I see you found our prize.'

'Yeah.'

'Who is he with?'

'Moses, an adopted uncle. Young Roy was staying with him in his cabin.'

'Darcy? Did he get away OK to Red Oak?'

Walt rubbed his hand across his neck. 'No, he did not.' Then slid his fingers across his jaw. 'He was shot down on the far side of the ridge. Ambushed by three scum from Tennessee. I thought you might have heard the shots.'

'No.' Sheriff Ireland's face set grimly as he shook his head. 'Shot down a sheriff. You know where they are from?'

'I do now. Pat Harrison, a known felon with an outstanding warrant.'

'The other two? I can have their names gazetted for apprehension.'

'They don't need gazetting, they're dead.'

'You were with him when he was shot?'

'No. He had left to return to Red Oak and was gunned down only minutes later. I followed and caught up with his assassins.'

'You did well.' The sheriff was still talking in a whisper.

'I could have done better had I got that lowlife Harrison, but I was also lucky. I stumbled across the three after they had left the ambush, and I was able to surprise them. I have Sheriff Townsend's star and the boy is wearing his rig.' Walt turned to see that Roy and Moses had closed up behind him, but both still remained mounted. 'Who was firing at you?'

'Don't know, but there were four of them. This little creek runs out about three miles up, so we came back down and that's when we were shot at. I yelled out, "Sheriff", but it seemed to make things worse.'

'Funny that,' said Walt.

'I didn't expect anyone to know about Red Oak, let alone Honey Creek.' The sheriff squeezed his eyes shut for a moment.

'Well, not so soon, maybe,' said Walt. 'But I knew they would get here eventually, that's the bush telegraph for you. The message just seems to pass through the air, somehow. But it is the local blacksmith at Red Oak who is putting out the word on Honey Creek, at twenty five dollars apiece.'

'How did he find out?'

'I got no idea, but I've seen it all before. You throw enough money around and even the dumbest son of a bitch gets to be as smart as a rat, and it never ceases to amaze me.'

Sheriff Ireland opened his eyes. 'So what now?'

'That's easy,' said Walt. 'We get out of here as quick as we can.'

'Have you got any idea how many we are up against?'

'I'd say all of those you spoke to in the community hall back in Bismarck, and then some.'

The sheriff's face looked grave.

Walt grinned. 'Hell, I was just kidding. It's still early days; be no more than fifty in these hills, I'd suspect. The rest won't arrive till tomorrow.'

Sheriff Ireland still didn't respond to Walt's humour. 'So where do we go? Going back to Red Oak is now impossible.'

'Nebraska,' said Walt. 'We need to head east to Omaha.'

'Then what?'

'We get the lawyer to buy us all a first-class rail ticket to Pennsylvania. You ever travelled first class?'

The sheriff looked surprised at the question and just shook his head without saying a word.

'Lordy, it's good. They even serve French champagne. Have you ever tried that?'

The sheriff squeezed his eyes shut again to relieve his headache and just shook his head in response.

36

SHOOT FIRST AND SHOOT STRAIGHT

The look on Sheriff Ireland's face was one part curiosity and two parts astonishment, as Walt explained his plan to take Justin Roy to meet Richard Tambling so that the offer of a reward could be rescinded.

The sheriff's response was that while he could see the intention of it all, he was unsure as to the outcome. 'Have you talked this over with Lawyer Harris?' he asked.

'Well no, not yet,' admitted Walt. 'But unless someone has a better idea, what other way is there?'

Sheriff Ireland hunched his shoulders. 'It's just that Tambling is. . .' the sheriff looked back up the small creek towards where the lawyer was hidden, 'a rich and powerful man, and he is also after blood. And I just don't think he'll even entertain a meeting with young Justin.'

Walt seemed to bristle. 'How much blood does he want? He's got the blood of a sheriff all over his hands. Had it not been for the reward Sheriff Townsend would not have been gunned down by trigger-happy lowlife trash.' Walt was starting to raise his voice. 'He's had all the blood he is going to get, and now he can pay for it.' Walt began to huff and puff a little.

The sheriff seemed to be taken somewhat aback by Walt's theatrics, but he wasn't swayed in his conviction that rich men always seemed to get their way. 'I hope you're right: that there'll be no more blood, but we aren't out of the woods yet, ourselves.'

Walt stopped blowing hard and settled a little.

The sheriff spoke quietly. 'I wish you luck, but I think it might be more certain if the reward was deemed unlawful and payment was forbidden in all states. If bounty chasers find that the reward can't be paid they'll stop chasing.'

Walt shook his head in disagreement. 'Just say you got some sort of federal deposition to make the payment illegal, right now, at this instant.' Walt snapped his fingers in the air. 'Do you think that would stop the likes of Richard Tambling from paying up? This whole proclamation shenanigans is about getting around the law. Making payment illegal would mean nothing to him. How do you stop the rich from spending their own money any way they see fit.' Walt was showing his frustration again.

'I telegramed Judge Maskell when the reward was posted. It was his court that tried the boy and he telegraphed back that he would move heaven and earth to have it deemed illegal. It may have happened already.'

'If it has,' said Walt, 'Then the word hasn't got into these hills, has it?'

The sheriff conceded that it had not. Then he said, 'I'm not saying don't go to Pennsylvania.'

'So what are you saying?'

'Just that the law should be given every opportunity to work.' Walt looked away as he spoke. 'I'll keep that in mind.'

Sheriff Ireland changed the subject. 'How do you propose we get out of here, in one piece?'

'What, apart from riding like hell?'

'Pretty much,' said the sheriff.

Walt turned and waved Moses and Justin Roy forward.

'We need to use a bit of local knowledge.'

Roy came forward first and extended his hand to Sheriff Ireland. 'Thank you for coming to look after me,' he said.

Sheriff Ireland looked a little embarrassed and seemed about to respond, but then just said, 'We need to keep our voices down. We got shot at an hour or two back.'

Walt looked at the young cowboy, observing the grace of his good manners, which was something he always admired, at least in others. But it was the look of reverence on his face that was the real surprise, as the young cowboy was showing his admiration for the sheriff; and for a fleeting moment Walt wondered if maybe he too was due a little veneration. After all, he was the one who had committed himself to the defence of the young man, albeit for a healthy commission.

But the feeling passed like the whisper of a cool breeze on a long hot night. 'Humph,' came the sound from Walt's lips before he said. 'This is Moses. He's a first-class scout.'

Sheriff Ireland shook Moses' large black hand. 'Moses,' he said with a nod.

Walt put the proposition to Moses. 'Can you get us out of these hills, so that we can make a run for the Nebraska state line?'

It could have been Moses' size, the way his large frame imposed itself upon their surroundings. Or maybe it was his eyes, which engaged with the confidence of a self-made man. Or even his deep warm voice. But whatever it was, Moses seemed to demand attention.

'From here we really only have one choice and that's straight back down Honey Creek. Up here we could easily get boxed in, and if we get caught in a gunfight, it will be a hold-down and that means we could take heavy casualties.'

Sheriff Ireland nodded in agreement.

'So we should take our chances,' continued Moses, 'and make a run for it. But in doing so we should protect the boy at all costs.'

Walt nodded. Protecting the boy meant protecting his commission.

'We must be a vanguard,' said Moses, 'and take any fire that is laid in his direction.'

Walt raised his eyebrows and had to stop himself from saying, *Oh, yeah?* out loud.

'But it has to be single file out of here; the track is narrow,' said Sheriff Ireland.

Moses nodded. 'Until we are on the flat, then we can protect the flanks.'

'You happy to show us the way out?'

Moses nodded to Sheriff Ireland.

'I'll follow you, then'll come Justin,' said the sheriff looking up at the young cowboy, 'then the lawyer, and Walt, are you happy to tail and defend us from anyone who may come up from behind?'

It suited Walt fine, as it would allow him to see where everybody was as they travelled out of the hills. 'Sure,' he said.

'And if we run into any hostility, then I guess we. . . .' the sheriff hesitated.

The pause allowed Walt to speak. 'Shoot first and shoot straight.'

37

DAMNED IF I KNOW

Walt didn't get to see Lawyer Harris until he emerged from the narrow gully of the tributary and came on to the track that ran beside Honey Creek. Moses had led them out and now stood guard as they got in line to leave, while Walt turned his mount to face upstream so that they would not be surprised by anyone coming down the trail. Justin Roy had led his horse into the shallows of the creek to make way for the sheriff to pass, and when the lawyer did come into view his face showed his concern. Walt greeted him with a small grin and a nod of his head, then walked his mount forward, to draw up alongside Harris and the young cowboy.

'This is Lawyer Harris,' said Walt softly. 'He has come from Pennsylvania to save you from harm.'

Roy snatched his hat from his head and whispered back, 'I am much obliged to you, Mr Harris.'

The acknowledgement and good manners seemed to perk the lawyer up a little, as he gave a faint smile. However, a large smudge upon his right cheek and dirt upon his coat showed that he had taken a recent tumble. His face reset into its original expression of grave concern. Walt had seen this look before, in the eyes of young men who had been shot at for the first time in their lives. It was a realization of vulnerability. Most men believe that misfortune will come only to the other man, but never to them. That is, until they have a close shave, and then they realize that such a belief is pure folly.

At a wave of the arm from Moses they set off at walking pace, with Walt weaving his horse from left to right across the trail where possible, to assist him in looking back up the trail for any danger. About an hour on, just as he was about to step his horse down a steep but short incline, Walt got the rare opportunity to actually see all of the other four riders at once. It was then that he caught sight of Moses as he raised a hand to halt all movement. Sheriff Ireland picked it up immediately and stopped, and so did the young cowboy, but the lawyer kept riding on, oblivious to the silent command. Walt clicked his tongue to get the attention of Lawyer Harris but, with his head down, the lawyer continued to step his horse carefully down the last part of the incline. Walt clicked his tongue again, twice, but the lawyer could not be diverted from his endeavours to traverse the rocky slop with care.

Walt glanced forward again to where he could see, some forty to fifty yards away, Moses slowly raising his shotgun to his shoulder. Walt eased himself up in the saddle just a little in an effort to see what Moses was aiming at, but he could see nothing, while the lawyer continued on, his horse's hoofs now starting to loosen bits of shale.

Stones rattled as they cascaded down the slope as Lawyer Harris, engrossed in the task at hand, brought his horse off the slope. Walt leant forward and slowly unsheathed his Winchester, then drew it into his shoulder. He had no aiming mark, but somewhere to the front of Moses, along a line from the muzzle of his double barrelled shotgun, lay the threat.

Lawyer Harris now looked up at Justin Roy, who had half-turned in the saddle in an effort to get the man's attention by waving his hand near his chest. The lawyer stopped, but seemed confused. He turned and looked back up at Walt, who was now in a firing position ready to engage the ground ahead of Moses.

The situation at last became clear to the lawyer. He let out a wail of, 'Oh my Lord,' just as the first shot was fired.

The lead round cracked through the trees over the heads of Moses, Sheriff Ireland, and Justin Roy. It passed by the lawyer, to thump into the top of the incline near the feet of Walt's mount.

The shot splintered shale, causing his horse to buck in surprise and step three or four paces to the right. This dislodged the butt of Walt's rifle from his shoulder, preventing him from laying down his first shot to where he believed the fire had come from. As he settled his horse with, 'Easy, easy,' he pushed his rifle back into his shoulder, just as Moses let the first barrel of the Stevens 10-gauge go.

In the rocky walled confines of the creek, it sounded like a small cannon. But that shot of authority did not deter their opponents; in fact it seemed to unleash a barrage of fire in their direction. Still Walt could see nothing, so he started to put down a methodical pattern of return fire over Moses' head and on to the ground in front of them, about eighty yards out. Moses let go the second barrel, then pulled his Army Colt from the holster and let three shots go in rapid fire. The sheriff dismounted and Justin Roy took his cue from the experienced lawman and followed suit, but he didn't draw the near-new nickel-plate Remington revolver that had once belonged to Sheriff Darcy Townsend of Red Oak.

Sheriff Ireland fired two shots, then pulled his rifle from his horse and advanced forward to Moses, while Walt continued with his fire, ensuring that he got a shot away every three or four seconds, to show that they were not a craven crew, about to run off. But as each of these shots passed over the lawyer's head, his horse became a little more unsettled, this was made worse as the rider was now pulling in every direction. Eventually his mount did what every smart horse does in such a situation; it reared up and dislodged its load, causing the lawyer to fall to the ground with a thump.

Through the thicket of young birch trees, Walt at last caught sight of movement, but it was no more than a fleeting dark shape of a rider turning his horse as he made his getaway. Walt let a shot go, but he missed and the target was gone. 'Damn,' he called, annoyed with himself and his poor luck. He dismounted with speed, to scurry down the rocky incline with his rifle in his left hand, his pistol in his right. As he passed the lawyer, still flat upon his back, he said with authority, 'Stay there.' On getting to the young cowboy, he called, 'Draw you pistol and guard the lawyer.' He then sprinted forward to take up a position to the right of Moses, who had also dismounted. 'How many?' he called.

'Three or four, not sure,' said Moses.

'At least three,' called the sheriff. 'But it could easily be four. Is everybody OK?'

'Fine,' said Walt. He started to advance down the side of the trail, his eyes fixed ahead.

Moses was down on one knee as he quickly reloaded his shotgun. 'Wait,' he said, 'I'll come with you.'

'Me too,' called the sheriff, but Walt told him to stay. 'Better you keep an eye back up the trail. The boy is looking after the lawyer. He took a tumble.'

Walt and Moses slowly advanced along the narrow path, weapons at the ready, each with eyes peeled for any sudden movement. The river then splashed to the left and both men turned their heads and guns towards the noise in an instant.

'Just fish,' whispered Moses.

As Walt looked back down the trail, his eyes caught sight of a spent cartridge on the ground. In the fading light it gleamed. He picked it up and he rolled it around in his fingers; the brass case was still warm to his touch. A little further up were more spent cases and marks upon the ground, where the horses had turned in their retreat.

'They're gone,' said Moses quietly.

'But where?' said Walt.

'There is only one way out from here, so they have gone back down the creek.'

'I know,' said Walt. 'They are now to our front on the only route out and the light is starting to fade. Looks awfully like an ambush situation to me.'

'What do you suggest we do?' asked Moses.

Walt kept looking straight ahead as he spoke. 'I was hoping

you were going to answer that for me, Moses, because I'm damned if I know.'

38

FROG IN A BOTTLE

When Walt returned up the trail he found Lawyer Harris still sitting upon the ground where he had fallen.

'How you doing?' he asked as he squatted down next to him.

'Walter, I've been shot at and thrown from my horse twice in the same day.' His words came slowly, along with a pained expression. 'Once was a shock, but twice is bewildering, absolutely bewildering. I don't know if my nerves can take it.'

'Well, it's not over yet.'

'You think there could be more?'

Walt paused before he spoke, as he didn't want to alarm the lawyer more than necessary. 'Well,' he said slowly, 'I think there could be more. . . .' he paused searching for the word.

'Altercations?' said the lawyer.

'No,' said Walt. 'More of an ambush than an altercation, I would have thought.'

The lawyer now looked alarmed. 'So how do we defend ourselves against such a deed?'

'Not sure,' said Walt, 'because there is only one way out of here and it's down this creek to the road. Once we cross that road, we will be on flat open ground, so we can spread out and ride fast all the way to Omaha, but up here we are a little like a frog in a bottle.'

'But hasn't Sheriff Townsend returned to Red Oak by a different path? Couldn't we use that?'

Walt bit at his tongue and it protruded a little over his bottom lip. Now was the time to advise the lawyer of what had happened to Sheriff Townsend, but he knew that he had a way of always seeming to say the wrong thing at the wrong time when it came to delicate matters. So he just said, 'No, too dangerous to go back to Red Oak, we need to go to Pennsylvania.' He stood up quickly and turned to walk back to Sheriff Ireland and Moses, leaving the lawyer to mouth the word Pennsylvania, silently.

The sheriff and Moses were kneeling on either side of the trail, acting as sentries. Walt knelt between them and placed the spent cartridge upright upon the ground. It was a bright .45 centre fire and new. 'These boys aren't running on the cheap,' he said.

Both the sheriff and Moses glanced down at the little empty cylinder.

'No reloads here, all new store bought ammunition,' continued Walt.

'Does that tell us anything?' asked the sheriff.

Walt pointed at the brass case. 'Well, it tells me they're serious, well stocked with good guns and ammunition, and smart, or lucky enough to have found us.'

'Could it be your man Harrison?'

'No, he's on his own. Still dangerous, mind, but those Tennessee boys were always half-arsed and tight. Would rather spend on liquor than store-bought ammunition. When Moses sprung these boys, they wouldn't have known who we were. That first shot was fired to see what we would do, and when we responded, they knew we weren't no local fishers and trappers out for recreation. We told them that we had something to protect, more than our hides.'

'If what you have added up is right, then how do we play this?' asked the sheriff.

'Well, the way I see it, we only have two choices,' said Walt. 'One is, we mount up, ride on and take our chances.'

The sheriff looked uneasy.

'If we do, then Moses and myself could ride ahead a way as scouts, then if we come across anyone, the boy should be out of the line of fire.'

'I don't know if I like that,' said Sheriff Ireland.

'I'm not selling its merits or otherwise,' said Walt, 'I'm just laying it before you as a choice.'

'Are you happy to do it?' asked the sheriff.

Walt scratched his chin. 'Was a time when I was young, it would have been exactly what I would have done, but nowdays it seems like a really dumb idea.'

'So, the other way?' asked Moses.

'We hold up here till it is dark then walk out, leading our horses. Once again with two out in front a way.'

The sheriff now rubbed his chin. 'What do you think, Moses?'

'I like the idea of waiting a little and going out in the dark on foot.'

'So do I,' said the sheriff. He looked back at Walt. 'It will give us some cover.'

'Me more than you,' said Moses with a smile.

'Now friend, they are true words,' said Walt nodding his head as if he had just received some wisdom from a pulpit. 'The rest of us should darken our faces like minstrels and muffle the horses.'

'How long will it take to walk out, Moses?' asked Sheriff Ireland.

'From here, travelling slow and sure, I'd say a good three hours.'

'So we should be down on the road well before midnight.'

'No,' said Walt. 'I say we don't leave till after midnight and aim to be down on the road an hour before first light. The longer we delay, then if they have laid an ambush they may tire and think that we have found another way out; they may become weary of the waiting.'

'That makes sense,' said the sheriff. 'Then we leave after midnight.'

'After midnight,' agreed Moses, his voice deep and melodic. 'And all looking like minstrels.'

39

PRAYER

The preparation for their precarious journey of stealth down Honey Creek began before last light, with the cutting of blankets to muffle the horse's hoofs. Moses worked with methodical and meticulous care, demonstrating to all his industrious nature. Here was a self-disciplined man. One who was in no need of supervision, as he could draw enthusiasm from the task alone. With the help of the young cowboy, he took each neat square mantle and attached it to a hoof with an elongated strip taken from the long side of the blanket, which then acted as binding around each lower leg.

Walt and the sheriff checked the saddlery of each of the horses in the fading light, running fingers over every brass buckle and stud to ensure that it would not ring out during their escape, while the lawyer hovered, watching with intense interest. Walt sensed that recent events had been a revelation to the attorney. Maybe it had exposed him to the raw realities of life, so Walt spoke quietly, explaining what he was doing, as if giving a lesson to a youth. It was not necessary. In fact, what he and the sheriff were doing was self-explanatory, but it involved the lawyer, and at that moment that was what was important.

With their bedrolls now chopped up, the five men sat upon the dirt in a small group, eating and sipping creek water from their cups. It was an unsatisfying meal and Walt would have stood on a street corner and sung a rendition of 'Onward, Christian Soldiers' for a hot coffee and a plate of beans. But the consensus was that they should have no fire and eat cold, so that no wafting cooking odours would give away their position. The sea biscuit that Walt chewed upon was on the stale side and reminded him of his Army service, so he turned his thoughts, instead, to the last time he'd felt the soft hand of a woman wash his back with sweet-smelling water. It was a brief and pleasant interlude.

As the dark descended and they prepared for the wait, the sheriff asked Walt if he wanted to run over the night's proceedings before they snatched some sleep. All eyes turned to Walt in anticipation. He had become their provisional leader, and while he was happy to hold an opinion on what needed to be done and direct others to do it, the formality of any such arrangement did not sit easily upon his shoulders. By nature and behaviour he was a man who preferred to work on his own and not be responsible for others.

He rubbed his chin and looked at the four faces in the closing light. Moses, his body leaning forward to show his eagerness to hear; Sheriff Ireland, relaxed with his rifle across his lap, waiting; Lawyer Harris, his clothes dusty and torn at the shoulder, but with an intense look in his eyes; and finally, Justin Roy, the young cowboy who was at the centre of this whole stunt. His young face contrasted sharply amongst those of the older men.

Walt rubbed his chin again, then slid his hand up over the back of his neck as he searched for the appropriate words. He looked up at their faces again.

'We leave on foot and the order will be Moses, me, Justin, Lawyer Harris and Sheriff Ireland. Keep sight of the horse to your front, but don't bunch up. If the horse in front stops, you stop. If it moves, you move. Moses will set the pace and it will be careful and slow. Speed is not of importance, but silence is.'

Moses was nodding his head in agreement. 'Noise is our enemy tonight,' he whispered.

I wish I'd said that, thought Walt as he nodded back to the big man. 'If they are lying in wait to ambush us, but are not vigilant, then with luck, we may pass by them undetected. But we must act as if we are close to danger at all times. So check and double check that all canteens are full and tops are on tight. A hollow sound will carry through the night air. Same with any items you pack in your valises, no loose tin cups or spoons to clatter or clang, metal on metal. Now try to get some shut-eye between your sentry shifts, but come up alert before we are ready to leave. No one can afford to be dozy.'

Walt was ready to say, *and that's it*, when the young cowboy asked. 'And if we get fired upon, what then?'

'Pray to the Lord that no such event should occur,' interjected the lawyer.

Walt thought for a moment, dismissing the reference to prayer, but stopping short of the urge to say flippantly that then they would all be on their way to hell in a hand-basket. 'Have your weapons ready and carry your rifles,' he said. 'If fired upon, return fire, then get on down the trail with speed, using your horse as a shield. Do not go back up the trail. We cannot afford to become split up. We will then regroup down the trail and out of range of any fire.'

'Sounds good to me,' said the sheriff.

'And if someone is wounded?'

'Then we will attend to their wounds,' said Walt to the young cowboy.

'But we have no dressings.'

Walt could feel himself getting annoyed. Did he have to think of everything?

'We have some blanket strips left over for plugging and binding,' said Moses.

'Good,' said Walt with relief. He glanced at Justin Roy to will him to stop asking questions.

It didn't work.

'Should we say a prayer?' Roy asked.

Walt could feel himself becoming very irritable, when Moses said to the young cowboy. 'Let me do that.'

'Thank you, Moses,' said Lawyer Harris.

Moses bowed his head and clasped his hands to his chest. 'Dear Lord, we seek your forgiveness for our sins and ask you to watch over us tonight and guide us out of these hills to safety. If you should so choose to call us to your kingdom tonight, may we go peacefully to your side and may you accept us into your house.' Moses paused with his head still bowed. 'Praise the Lord. Amen.'

All repeated, 'Amen', except Walt. He was not a religious man and felt no need for such a custom. However, he had always been curious as to how others found succour in prayer. He sometimes wondered if he was missing out on something. Walt came out of his private thoughts as Moses extended his hand towards Walt.

'You are a good man,' said Moses as his strong grip wrapped around Walt's hand.

'Hear, hear,' said the sheriff, echoed by the lawyer and the young cowboy.

Walt didn't know what to say, and his face showed that he was a little stunned.

40

TRAP

They left an hour after midnight, according to the lawyer's pocket watch, but he said it could be a little slow from the two falls he had recently taken. A small crack had appeared on the glass just near the bottom of the dial. It was a telltale wound to a fine timepiece, and it now recorded that hard day.

'How are you feeling?' asked Walt, making no more than small talk.

'As if I have been dragged down Main Street behind a beer wagon,' came the response.

It seemed an odd reference to make, the one of the beer wagon, but the lawyer was using frivolity at a time of seriousness and Walt appreciated the effort. 'I've had that feeling,' he whispered back. 'Like every bone in your body has been whacked for good measure, but it passes.'

'When?' asked the lawyer.

'No time at all,' said Walt. Then he added 'Just a month or two,' to return the good humour.

They moved off at a slow walk in file, but stopped about one hundred yards down the trail. The problem was small, but a remedy was necessary. A worn saddle-bag buckle on the lawyer's mount clinked in step with his horse. The sheriff found the troublesome buckle and threaded the end of the leather strap back through the brass frame to hold it tight. Lawyer Harris was apologetic, but there was no need, not at least to Walt, as he knew that such a small sound was almost beyond his hearing. He just hoped that all the buckles he had checked were silent.

The method of communicating in the dark, in single file, between each man in the group required small calls to draw attention to the man in front to stop. This was quickly seen as dangerous, and needed to be sorted out with speed. The sheriff suggested that they rope the horses together and that they walk with a hand upon the rope leading back to the horse behind. Except of course, for Moses, who was leading the team. Should one of them then wish to draw attention to the man in front he could pull on the line or even walk forward to the next man, while the horses would remain in position in single file.

It took about twenty minutes to rig the horses and another twenty minutes to test their ploy by stopping and starting with pulls on the rope. When finally they were ready to proceed the lawyer squinted at the face of his watch in the dark and thought that it said just after two. Walt guessed that was about right. They had lost an hour and covered not more than 300 yards. With at least seven and half miles to go, it was now doubtful if they would make the road before first light. This was of concern, as he had hoped to be out of the hills by then.

By three o'clock Walt calculated that they had covered two miles, a speed that reflected their caution and ability to remain near silent. By four, they had travelled another two miles, with three and half miles to go and less than two hours of darkness. It was going to be touch and go if they were to make it out of the hills under the full cover of darkness. But they were now over the halfway mark and in a steady routine, moving towards their goal and making little noise except for the muffled steps of the horses. Walt allowed himself the indulgence of relaxing, just a little.

It was when the first streaks of grey started to mark the coming of first light that Moses stopped abruptly. Walt pulled up and waited, expecting to start again at any moment, but the horse to his front stood perfectly still, as if it were a statue. As the minutes passed, Walt expected Moses to appear before him to explain the cause of their delay, but he didn't emerge from the dark and Walt could feel himself becoming agitated.

After three or four minutes of waiting Walt moved forward. He found Moses standing in front of his horse with his shotgun at the ready. As he went to whisper his enquiry as to the interruption, Moses put his fingers to Walt's lips to silence him. He then took his hand and guided it to settle gently upon a taut rope that had been stretched across the narrow trail. To the right ran the creek, which made a soft bubbling sound, and to the left was a thicket of dark brush, where Moses had been pointing his double barrels.

Walt felt the warmth of Moses's breath against his ear as he whispered, 'Trap.'

Walt's heart was now racing. Moses had, by good measure or

good fortune, found the trap that had been set for them. Had they been riding fast, this line would have brought down the first horse and rider, but that was not what Walt believed was its purpose. This line was to provide early warning, to alert those in waiting over that long night, that the prey had entered the snare. Walt slowly ran his hand along the tight line to the left and it touched upon an empty tin can, its lid pulled back so that it could loop over the rope. If dislodged to fall upon the ground, the subsequent noise would stir those in ambush who must now be dozing just before the dawn. He slid his hand to the right and found two more cans, which he gently lifted from the rope. The first smelt of fish and the second of condensed milk.

Walt turned his head slowly and glanced back up the single file; he was able to make out the shapes of the horses. First light was starting to take hold. He had to do something and do it quickly or they were all going to be seen. He had no idea exactly where the ambush lay. He suspected that they were on the flank of the trap, but they could also be standing in the very middle of the ground that had been chosen for their death. *It makes no difference* he told himself. *The trap has been set and we are in it, but it is not yet sprung.*

Walt now took Moses's hand and placed it upon the tight line. As the big man bent forward, Walt whispered, his lips almost brushing against the ear. 'Can you hold the line while I cut it?'

Moses didn't answer; he just placed his Stevens 10-gauge shotgun gently upon the ground, so that he could bring two hands to bear upon the rope.

Once in position, Walt asked. 'Ready?'

Moses took in a deep breath, then nodded his head.

Walt could now see the stretched rope clearly in the pale light as he searched his pockets for his folding knife.

Moses whispered. 'Ready,' as he clutched the rope tight in his hands, prepared to take up the strain when it was cut.

'Can't find my damn pocket knife,' whispered Walt as he fished around in his pockets.

142

'Mine,' said Moses. 'Top right pocket. Pull back on the blade easy, it's as sharp as a razor.'

Walt placed his Winchester upon the ground and felt into Moses's shirt pocket to extract a small bone-handle folding knife that was not much more than three inches long. He grasped the back of the blade and pulled the cutting edge out with a click, to reveal a clean, well-oiled cutting edge.

'Ready,' said Moses again as he sucked in another breath.

Walt placed the razor-sharp edge against the straining rope and drew it back. The strands of the taut rope peeled back as the fine steel sliced through the tight line. The speed with which the rope separated surprised Walt. It seemed to cut with no effort. Moses gripped tight, his arms bulging. The line broke, the ends springing apart, but only by no more than the length of the knife. Moses had tentative control over the two ends, but to lose his grasp now would result in a recoil, like a sharp spring, and it would awake their enemy.

Walt brought his free hand down upon the rope to help ease it back slowly, but he soon realized that his contribution was of little consequence. Moses was taking all the strain as bit by bit, he was able to relieve the tension on the line. The look upon the big man's face was of intense concentration, as little by little he wrestled the rope to the ground. Walt watched with admiration, not just at his sheer physical strength, but also at his ability to execute such a delicate manoeuvre. He laid the two ends of the rope upon the ground; they were now separated by nearly four feet.

Walt patted Moses's shoulder, then leant in close to whisper. 'We've got to go quick and quiet.'

Moses said nothing, the sweat glistening upon his skin as it ran down the side of his face.

When Walt got back to his horse he could see the outline of the other three all standing in line with their blackened faces, waiting and watching. He gave a wave to indicate that they were ready to go and realized that he still had Moses's folding knife in his hand. He closed the blade and dropped it into his trouser pocket, before raising two fingers to run under his neck to indicate danger. He then put his fingers to his lips and pointed to the left of the track.

The three heads nodded back to indicate that they had got his message, just as his horse started to move forward on its tether to follow Moses.

Walt drew in a breath and gripped his Winchester tight in his left hand, then placed his right hand upon the rope leading back to the young cowboy's horse.

When they were at least fifty yards on from that cut rope, Walt allowed himself some comfort that they had passed the immediate danger. It was then that the first shot rang out in the drab pastel light of that early morning, and he felt himself jump with fright.

41

GO

Walt slapped the rump of his horse and yelled, 'Go,' then stepped back, turning to face the three who had been behind him. 'Go,' he yelled again to Justin Roy, who for that moment seemed to have frozen solid. A second shot rang out, then a third and fourth, and each time the young man ducked his head instinctively, even though he was still shielded by the horses. More shots followed, one passing directly over Walt's head, then one thumped into the last horse, causing it to rear in distress.

Justin Roy was now moving, but Walt gave him another hurry-up as he passed. 'Go, go.' He waved to the lawyer to follow on, continuing to call, 'Go, go.' The tethered horses were also now on the move, signalling that Moses had got his horse going and the others were now following, their muffled hoofs stomping upon the ground as they tried to get traction.

A shot from their group rang out at last. It was the sheriff, now exposed and kneeling on the trail as he returned fire. As the last horse passed Walt, churning dust, he raised his rifle to his shoulder and standing, let go three rapid shots into the ambush, which was to the left of the trail and back about thirty yards.

'Let's go,' he yelled to the sheriff, who fired one more shot, then came to his feet, turned, took one step and collapsed to fall heavily upon the ground.

Walt let go two more shots, then sprinted towards the crumpled shape of the sheriff some ten yards away; as he ran shots struck the ground around his feet to show that their attackers had found their range. Walt grabbed at the sheriff's jacket, just near the back of the collar, and with a fistful of fabric, he pulled.

The sheriff rolled over to face upward and his rifle fell from his hands. Walt reached down and tried to scoop up the Winchester while still holding his own rifle. He fumbled, then clenched both hot barrels near the muzzles, just as a bullet pierced the sleeve of his coat above the elbow. He looked down at the hole and although he felt no wound he expected to see blood; none came. The bullet had missed his arm, but by no more than a fraction of an inch.

As the shots from the ambush struck upon the trail kicking up dust, Walt pulled with all his might, dragging the wounded sheriff towards safety. When he was some thirty yards down the track, leaving two long grooves in dirt from the sheriff's dragging heels, he glanced up to see Moses running towards him. He had his shotgun held across his chest and had come back to assist. Walt's spirits immediately began to lift and he felt the extra energy he needed to pull Sheriff Ireland from the line of fire.

Moses dashed past Walt some dozen paces then stopped, lifted his 10-gauge to his shoulder and, still standing, let both barrels go, one after the other with only seconds to spare. The sound of the big-bore gun seemed to echo back up the valley like rolling thunder.

Walt continued to pull, glancing forward where he had to go, then glancing back at Moses who was now pulling his ancient Colt from his holster.

'Moses, get back,' yelled Walt, as he continued to pull the sheriff to safety. Then he looked forward again and saw the bend in the track where the river turned to the right, close to the gully wall that offered protection. He glanced back to see Moses, still standing, his shotgun clasped in his left hand by his side, his pistol in his right, arm extended as he took aim and fired. 'Moses,' yelled Walt again, but the word seemed to catch in his mouth as he tried to suck air into his heaving lungs. 'Moses,' he tried once more, and this time the word came out as no more than a wheeze, as he tried to catch his breath. Now almost spent, Walt saw a hand reach down and grasp the collar of the sheriff's jacket, close to his hand. It was Lawyer Harris. The dead weight of the sheriff seemed to diminish as if by magic as the body lifted a little and they scrambled with increased speed to the safety of the small embankment.

As Walt fell backwards upon the ground, totally exhausted, the sheriff's head in his lap, he caught sight of a figure rushing by. It was the young cowboy going to the aid of Moses Carter.

'Oh, geezes,' said Walt aloud. 'Why did he have to go and do that?' He pulled himself from under the sheriff. 'Stay here,' he shouted to the lawyer, 'and don't move. Find the wound, plug it and wait.' He rolled to his feet and stood; light-headed he staggered a little, then took off after Justin Roy.

The images of the young cowboy and the big Negro jerked before Walt's eyes like string puppets as he ran towards them. Their figures silhouetted in the early-morning light and a haze of dust. In his ears came the sound of gunshots as they cracked over his head or thumped into the ground to kick up dirt and dust.

Walt's lungs burnt as if a white-hot branding iron had been plunged down into his chest. His legs felt heavy as if weighed down by lead and his feet seemed to be made of wood. And in his mind was an almost overwhelming fear that at any moment a rifle bullet would strike him with a fierce thud.

Walt didn't see that precise moment when Moses was wounded. He had seen the big man standing and the young cowboy running. Then, when he looked again, Moses had turned, his big hand gripping at his side and clenching a fist full of bloodstained shirt. Justin pushed himself up under Moses's arm to support him from falling and Walt arrived to do the same on the other side of the big man. The weight upon Walt's shoulder was immense, but from an unknown source he seemed to find the necessary strength, and the three, linked together, with their backs to their assassins, scrambled back down the narrow trail.

With each step Walt expected to feel the impact of a bullet in his back, but by mercy or luck it never came, and as Walt staggered with jolting footsteps, he found himself mumbling a childhood prayer that he thought he had long forgotten.

42

LUCKY DAY

The sheriff was sitting up, his face pale and drawn, his right leg bloodied on the side of the thigh where he had been struck by a round. The lawyer had plugged the wound and bound it with blanket strips. Although wounded, the patient was fully conscious and holding his Winchester, which rested upon his lap.

Moses was in worse shape. His wound was to the left side at the waist. The bullet had missed the hip, which would have fractured and splintered the bone, and fortunately it had also missed the ribcage and the lower part of the lungs. However, it had entered that part of the body where vital organs and intestines lie. Lawyer Harris lifted Moses' hand from his side where he had gripped his injury, and placed three layers of cut blanket there, then reapplied his bloodied hand, to press down and stem the flow of blood, while he prepared to bind the wound.

'Can you two ride?' asked Walt. 'Because we need to break out of here, if we don't get away from these hills we'll be cut off and cut down.'

The sheriff started to rise, as Moses said in a deep voice, 'Yes sir.'

'We'll help you mount, but you will have to hang on until we can get across the road and are on flat ground. Then we may be able to ease up.'

The sheriff grimaced as he came to his feet and stumbled a little before Lawyer Harris held him steady.

'We'll get you up first, Sheriff, then Moses.' Walt leant in close so that Sheriff Ireland could grip his shoulder for support.

Getting the sheriff into the saddle was done with relative ease, even though he was only able to use one leg. But mounting Moses was a different story. It took the strength of all three fit men to lift him up. Walt pushed his shoulder under Moses' rump and felt the big man grimace and shake with pain. Once Moses was mounted Walt stood for a moment to catch his breath and saw blood upon the front of his jacket near the shoulder. It was a heavy stain, wet and warm, which meant that Moses was leaking bad.

'Ride east into the sun as hard as you can,' said Walt to the young cowboy. 'It will give the sheriff and Moses the direction.'

'The sheriff's horse has been hit.'

'I know,' said Walt. 'Double mount if needs be. If you can't manage that, stay with the sheriff. I'll be along soon. Now go.'

The cowboy made as though to say something.

Walt just said, 'Go,' then turned away to face back up the trail as he went down on to one knee and began reloading his rifle.

Just as he got the last cartridge into the loading port and the sound of the departing riders had faded away, he saw five riders emerge from the brush. One was bent forward, cradling his arm, but Walt was unsure as to the seriousness of his wound. He raised his Winchester to the shoulder and, still kneeling, lined up the leading man and fired.

His first round struck the target, toppling the rider to the ground. The other four riders scattered with three returning to the cover of the brush and one breaking to Walt's left and into the creek bed, to splash back upstream and out of sight. Walt continued to lay down fire in both directions, knowing that a hit would just be plain luck, but he had surprise on his side, and wanted to leave his foes with the impression that they were up against a larger force, which had now bunkered down behind the embankment.

Walt fired three more rapid shots, turned, then made a run for his horse. As he mounted and stretched out his left arm to hold the saddle horn, he noticed a second bullet hole in his clothing. This time it was near the bottom of the sleeve. It had been his lucky day, but was his good fortune going to last?

He had trouble bringing his horse to a gallop as the gelding kept turning to the side. Walt booted hard to get a response, then he realized that the muffling of the hoofs was now a problem. He dismounted, looking back up the trail and expecting to see riders bearing down upon him as he pulled at the blanket strips. One had already fallen off completely and the two on the rear hoofs had become displaced, but were still hanging from the lower leg. The one at the front left was still bound tight and the knots were hard to move. Walt continued to pull and curse, while each second or two he glanced back up the trail.

'Come on, you mongrel,' he called to the binding. 'Get off there.' Then he remembered Moses's knife in his pocket. He pulled the blade free and ran the back of the cutting edge down the side of the fetlock towards the hoof, then flicked it out at the blanket strips, which fell away as if let go by an unseen hand. Walt flicked the blade closed, then, looking back up the trail, he grabbed at his saddle horn and mounted. Just as he landed in the seat of the saddle and dug his heels in to his horse, the knife dropped from his hand. He took off, then pulled back on the reins.

Why, when he was outnumbered and close to danger, did he go back for that folding knife that belonged to Moses? Even Walt couldn't answer that, but go back he did, dismounting, fetching it up to put in his pocket before riding off again.

Walt tried to push his horse to a gallop, only to find that the trail narrowed and turned sharply to the right, then dropped down sharply over rocky ground. Upon the path were pieces of discarded blanket and it took the best part of another mile before the ground became flat and the trail widened. Then, in less than a hundred yards it narrowed again for a quarter of a mile. Walt cussed as the brush encroached on either side and a small branch smacked him in the face. Then, when he had become most annoyed at the obstacles, the trail widened and before him was the road and open ground.

It took Walt another two miles to catch up to the young cowboy, the lawyer, the sheriff, and Moses. When he did he was impressed at the distance they had covered, but it had taken its toll on the wounded. The sheriff's face was bleach-white, while Moses had a faraway stare in his eyes as he gripped at his side.

They rode on for another three miles into the rising sun with Walt constantly glancing back, before he saw the dust behind them. They were now being chased on open ground and the gap was closing as their speed had slowed from a gallop to a canter. Walt began looking for a place to hide, but out here, away from the hills, there was little on offer. His mind raced as he considered the few choices available to him. If they rode on, they would eventually be run down. If they stopped in the open, they would be gunned down. If Walt was to turn and attack, he would cause a delay but no more, as the pursuers outgunned him. The only answer was to stop and fight, but they needed ground in their favour to do that.

Walt rode ahead, calling back to each rider, 'We are being run down, we have to stand and fight, but we need cover. Look for cover.'

The message made no impression on the wounded and the look of confusion on Lawyer Harris's face showed that he had no idea what to look for in suitable ground. But Justin Roy nodded his head and immediately sat erect in the saddle, looking from side to side. Walt caught the calm on his face and the determination in his eyes. He was showing grit and it would be needed.

Another mile passed and the heat of the early-morning sun was upon their faces, bringing beads of sweat that now streaked through the dirt they had applied to their skin.

'There,' called the cowboy.

Walt looked, but could see nothing.

'There, to the right front, low brush.'

Walt saw it. Some squat, scrubby brush, some 200 yards away, which seemed to offer little in the way of cover.

The cowboy turned towards the shrubbery undergrowth and Walt was just about to say no, keep due east, when he realized that he was just seeing the tops of the foliage, which meant the ground dipped.

'Lord, give us somewhere to stand and fight,' came his prayer. 'Just a little cover so that we are not gunned down in the open like dogs.'

Maybe it was more a plea than a prayer, but Walt, a man who never went to church, had at that moment called upon a higher being for help.

The dip in the ground was a dry sandy creek-bed with banks no more than three feet high, which broke away and crumbled under the horses' hoofs. Walt galloped ahead down the dry bed that now turned north. Some eighty yards up was the brush that Justin Roy had seen. It stood about eight feet tall and, while not perfect, it would hide the horses and it offered the best cover available. Walt pulled his horse to a halt, turned in the saddle and waved to the four following riders.

'Dismount,' he called, 'and get against the bank.'

The young cowboy immediately went to Moses to help and the lawyer went to assist the sheriff. Walt pulled his rifle from its scabbard and raced back down the dry creek bed to sight their assailants. As he watched he reloaded his Winchester, and guessed that the oncoming riders were not more than a mile from their position and therefore only minutes away. He turned and raced back to the group to find the sheriff and Moses slumped with their backs against the soft dirt bank; both of them looked in a bad way. The cowboy was holding a water canteen to Moses's lips but he was having trouble drinking.

'Arm up and shoot anything that comes down this way,' said Walt. Then he added, 'Except me.'

'What are you going to do?' asked Lawyer Harris.

'Shoot them before they shoot me,' said Walt. He grabbed a water canteen and headed back up the old dry creek bed towards the attackers.

43

THE BATTLE

The battle that took place that morning was heard but not seen by the four who huddled against the earth bank of the dry creek bed. The sheriff told the lawyer, through drawn lips, that while there was shooting it meant that Walt was putting up a good fight.

'I should go and help,' said Lawyer Harris.

'And do what?' asked the sheriff. 'Stay here. Our fight will come soon enough.'

It was then that the lawyer realized that if the fight was to come to them, it would be at the cost of Walt's life, and that thought was almost enough to paralyse him with fear. His only movements came from the repeated noise of each rifle and pistol shot, which made his body jerk, as if being pulled by invisible strings. Then a round landed close with a thump into the sand immediately in front of them, as the intensity of the shooting heightened, and the lawyer's apprehension could now be seen on his face as it contorted as if in pain.

When the sound of fire that had filled the still morning air stopped abruptly, and quiet was restored, there came also an eerie sense of anticipation. Each minute that passed seemed to be agonizingly drawn out, before the sheriff said, 'Our turn is about to come.'

But the minutes continued to pass and still no one appeared. Then one single shot was heard. The sound rolled down the hollow like a starter's gun for a foot race at a carnival, and it made the lawyer lurch as the air expelled from his lungs.

'Be ready boys,' said the sheriff. 'Here they come.'

Still the minutes ticked by as the silence held, before a lone figure came down the sandy creek bed with a Winchester in his left hand and a Colt in his right. It was Walt and his walk was slow, like that of a tired man with heavy feet. As he approached it could be seen that he was covered in dust from head to toe, which caught the morning sun and gave off a golden glow.

'My canteen has a couple of holes in it,' he said. 'Anyone got any water?'

The lawyer sprang to his feet and fetched a half-full canteen from one of the horses. 'What happen?' he asked as he handed

Walt the container.

But Walt didn't answer his question. He just said, 'We've got to go.'

However, only four departed. Moses had passed on as he lay propped up against the earth embankment with his eyes staring into the distance towards the east. His death affected the young cowboy profoundly. His tears flowed uncontrolledly and he wanted the big man's body to be taken with them across the state line and into Omaha. Fortunately, the sheriff was able to dissuade him from this idea, saying that his body would have to be brought back to Iowa for burial, and carrying a body back and forth, while hanging over a horse, was undignified.

'The law will have to recover Sheriff Townsend's body and return him to Red Oak, they can recover Moses as well,' he said. Then he added, 'I will see to it myself.'

It was only then that Lawyer Harris learnt of the death of Sheriff Darcy Townsend of Red Oak. It seemed to strike him like a blow to the stomach which bent him over, before he drew in some long breaths and stood upright.

He was to never ask Walt as to the circumstances of Sheriff Townsend's death, and Walt was never to offer an account. Two of their small band had died, while one had received a serious wound to his leg, but he and the boy had survived against the odds, and they owed it all to Walter Garfield, an aging ex-US Marshal with a cantankerous disposition, a disrespectful manner, and an immeasurable well of courage.

The lawyer had seen a side of human nature that he had not known to exist. It was both good and bad, but it had educated him in a way that he would never have believed possible.

When they crossed Missouri River into Nebraska later that day, on the Lone Tree flat boat, their small group stood around the wounded sheriff, who remained mounted upon his wounded horse. Not a word passed between them, but the lawyer felt like a very different man, and a brother to these men of the West.

The sheriff was admitted to the Omaha state infirmary and

operated upon that same evening to have a .44 bullet removed from his leg. The surgeon, who had served under General Samuel Sturgis at the Battle of Wilson's Creek, believed that the round must have struck a small tree before slowing just enough to lodge in the leg without exiting, thereby limiting the damage. A graze on the nose of the bullet supported his assertion.

On the Union Pacific train journey to Pennsylvania the young cowboy, the lawyer and Walt fell into exhausted silence, but sleep for all three was fitful, with each experiencing dreams of doom that snapped them awake.

On arrival at Pittsburgh, Lawyer Harris announced that Walt and the young cowboy should stay with him in his house, which was close to the conservatory and botanical gardens. Walt didn't much care where it was as he had no intention of visiting either, but the invitation did mean that he would not have to pay for a second-rate boarding house, and to him that sounded like a good deal.

The following morning the three arose, washed, and then sat down at a linen covered table to a breakfast of ham and eggs, before the lawyer announced that they should prepare for a visit to meet with Mr Richard Standley Tambling.

44

HE'S GOT A GUN

The lawyer was dressed in a long frock-coat and a top hat. Justin Roy was most impressed with the transformation, as Lawyer Harris had looked somewhat threadbare of late, from his travels in the Wild West. However, Walt was only mildly impressed as he had never been one to put too much stock in clothing as a representation of the man. What he did notice was the look of the lawyer's face, as his cheeks had slightly depressed, giving him a gaunt look. Lawyer Harris did say that he had lost considerable weight over the past weeks, so was thankful that his suspenders were able to hold up his trousers, and Walt took the jocular remark to be a sign of good spirits.

The lawyer had arranged, on the previous day via a telephone call by his butler, for a travelling apparel salesman to visit. From his carriage the man produced a range of off-the-peg garments. Most of the clothing was for city living and included the latest in striped trousers, coloured waistcoats and frock-coats. Lawyer Harris purchased two white dress shirts and Walt selected a check pattern wool suit that looked somewhat out of place with his hat and boots, but he had no eye for fashion and thought it to be a smart selection. The young cowboy chose a charcoal-grey suit with a blue pinstripe which, like Walt's attire, came at the benevolence of Lawyer Harris.

As they prepared to leave, Walt told Roy to put on Sheriff Ireland's rig.

'Why?' he asked.

'Because we need to look businesslike,' said Walt as he strapped on his own rig.

Lawyer Harris said nothing.

As they left Walt picked up a large orange from the fruit bowl on the sideboard and placed it in the outer pocket of his coat. The bulge it made looked odd, but Walt seemed not to notice.

When they entered Richard Tambling's house with its huge entry, high ceilings and grand staircase, the cowboy's mouth opened with amazement; he had never seen any house so grand. He looked down upon the black-and-white-tiled floor and slowly shook his head. 'It is like those photographs I've seen of a city hotel foyer,' he said.

They were shown into the library with its wall-to-ceiling shelves of books, while the lawyer left to speak to Tambling. Walt eased himself into a dark-leather chair and dropped his hat upon his knee, then pulled Moses's small folding knife from his trouser pocket and began carefully to peel his orange. The young cowboy stood to the side of the large room and fidgeted as he looked at the books.

The wait annoyed Walt, as it seemed to go on for ever, and he guessed the delay could only mean one thing, that the discussions between Harris and Tambling, on the removal of the bounty on Justin Roy's head, had stalled. This was confirmed when the double doors of the library were thrown open and Richard Tambling, whose face was flushed red with anger, entered in a rush, followed by Lawyer Harris.

'I will have no deputation forced upon me in my house to tell me what I can or can't do,' he bellowed at Walt.

Walt stood, his eyes narrowing with contempt as he looked over the old man. He then switched his gaze to the lawyer, and was ready to give him a similar look for allowing this tirade to be foisted upon him.

However, Lawyer Harris stepped forward. 'Richard,' he said in a firm and clear voice that came with authority. 'This is Walter Garfield. I hired him to protect the man you sought to destroy.'

'You had no right,' said Tambling. 'My instructions were clear. If the law won't deliver justice then I will do it myself.'

'But you weren't doing it yourself,' said Lawyer Harris. 'You just paid others to do it for you, and by doing so the lives of two good men have been lost and another has been seriously wounded.'

'I will have my justice. I will have my revenge.' Tambling's head was shaking and his lips were trembling with rage. 'I will see the man who killed my son burn in hell for the cowardly act upon my boy.'

'It was not a cowardly act,' said Justin Roy.

Tambling turned his gaze to the young man. 'Who are you?'

Walt instinctively bent at the knees, just slightly, as if ready for a fight. He could not believe that Lawyer Harris had not informed Tambling that the man who killed his son was now in his house.

'This is Justin Roy,' said Harris, his voice still firm. 'He is the young man who shot your boy, but he did so with cause and has been acquitted by a court of law of any wrongdoing.'

'What!' yelled Tambling.

Roy went to speak, but he couldn't be heard above the ranting outburst from Richard Tambling, who then turned and stormed out of the library.

'I have failed,' said Lawyer Harris.

Walt agreed, but said nothing while Justin Roy remained rigid, dumbfounded and cemented to the spot.

Tambling reappeared at the door.

The young cowboy saw the old man, and in a gesture of good will advanced towards him, his hand outstretched. 'I ask for your forgiveness,' he said.

Walt caught the cold look upon Tambling's face and started to follow Roy across the room.

'I have regretted my actions every day since,' continued the young cowboy.

'Forgive? Never!' yelled Tambling.

Just as the young cowboy was within a pace of this viciously angry old man, Tambling spat directly in the face of Justin Roy, almost at the same time that Lawyer Harris called out. 'He's got a gun.'

45

NICE

A trigger squeezed and a hammer flew forward, striking the base of a cartridge. The shot exploded from the end of the muzzle in a flash of flame and smoke, causing both Lawyer Harris and Justin Roy to jump with fright, as Richard Standley Tambling stood erect and still for just a moment. His eyes registered the blinding flash, but it is not known if his ears heard the booming blast. The small, spinning lead bullet struck him just below the bridge of the nose, punching a small neat hole in the skull, severing the optic nerve, passing through the temporal lobe, to explode the cerebellum as it exited from the back of his head. The energy from the force of the shot smashed the skull like a porcelain bowl dropped upon a stone floor. One piece, about the size of a child's hand and with skin and hair still attached, flew across the room to land upon a reading table and rest amongst a small pile of books.

Walter Douglas Garfield did not flinch or jump. He had fired the shot from an instinctive fast draw while standing behind and just to one side of Justin Roy. The path of the bullet from his gun had passed over Roy's shoulder to slice through the air less than one inch from the side of his face, before it then struck its intended target.

Tambling's body dropped to the floor. On his face was a look of absolute astonishment, with wide staring eyes. His left hand was twisted and obscured behind his back from the fall, but his right hand was outstretched, away from the side of the body for all to see.

'He was armed,' came a voice of shock. It was Lawyer Harris.

Their eyes looked down at the hand that still held the dark frame of a revolver, then to the outstretched left leg that began to jump slightly and rap-tap-tap upon the floor. This wretched little jig was the dance of death.

Walter put his hand upon Justin Roy's shoulder, then stepped past him to kneel close to the body. He looked down at the pistol, leaning forward and squinting a little. 'Colt Frontier,' he said. 'Nice.' He looked back at the young cowboy. 'Looks new, not a scratch on it. Could have shot you dead. He was concealing it under his coat.'

'I saw it,' said Roy.

'You did?' said Walt. 'Then why didn't you shoot?'

The response was stuttered. 'I couldn't shoot. I just didn't have it in me.'

Walt didn't respond, at least not to the declaration that the young cowboy had just made; he saw no need. What he did do was pull from his trouser pocket the small folding knife that had belonged to Moses Carter. 'Here,' he said. 'Before I forget, this is for you. It belonged to Moses.'

'I didn't have the courage,' said the cowboy, still gazing upon the body.

Walt waved the pocket knife at the young man to get his attention. 'Take it,' he said.

Justin Roy slowly took the knife. 'I didn't have the courage to shoot,' he repeated.

'Had nothing to do with courage.' Their fingers touched as the knife was taken. 'You went back for Moses, now that took courage. You've just had your fill of killing. But now you're free of all that. A dead man's proclamation goes with him to the grave.'

The cowboy looked at the pocket knife, then slowly put it in his pocket and undid the buckle on Sheriff Darcy Townsend's gun belt. As it came loose he handed it to Walt, who ran his eye over the Remington with the black grips.

'Now that is a nice handpiece, made from the finest polished American steel,' he said. 'Nice. Real nice.'